THE

LIVING

END

A Henry Robbins Book  E. P. DUTTON · NEW YORK

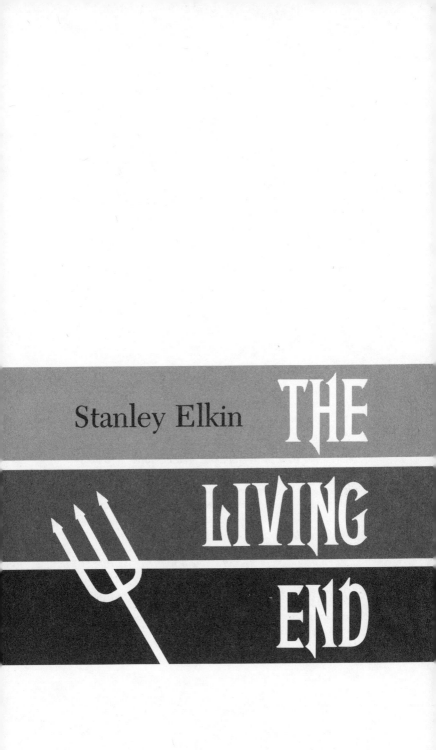

Stanley Elkin

THE
LIVING
END

To Joan

Part I THE

CONVENTIONAL

WISDOM

llerbee had been having a bad time of it. He'd had financial reversals. Change would slip out of his pockets and slide down into the crevices of other people's furniture. He dropped deposit bottles and lost money in pay phones and vending machines. He overtipped in dark taxicabs. He had many such financial reversals. He was stuck with Super Bowl tickets when he was suddenly called out of town and with theater and opera tickets when the ice was too slick to move his car out of his driveway. But all this was small potatoes. His portfolio was a disgrace. He had gotten into mutual funds at the wrong time and out at a worse. His house, appraised for tax purposes at many thousands of dollars below its replacement cost, burned down, and recently his once flourishing liquor store, one of the largest in Minneapolis, had drawn the attentions of burly, hopped-up and armed deprivators, ski-masked, head-stockinged. Two of his clerks had been shot, one killed, the other crippled and brain damaged, during the most recent visitation by these marauders, and Ellerbee, feeling a sense of responsibility, took it upon himself to support his clerks' families. His wife reproached him for this, which led to bad feeling between them.

"Weren't they insured?"

"I don't know, May. I suppose they had some insurance but how much could it have been? One was just a kid out of college."

"Whatshisname, the vegetable."

"Harold, May."

"What about whosis? He was no kid out of college."

"George died protecting my store, May."

"Some protection. The black bastards got away with over fourteen hundred bucks." When the police called to tell him of the very first robbery, May had asked if the men had been black. It hurt Ellerbee that this should have been her first question. "Who's going to protect you? The insurance companies red-lined that lousy neighborhood a year ago. We won't get a penny."

"I'm selling the store, May. I can't afford to run it anymore."

"Selling? Who'd buy it? *Selling!*"

"I'll see what I can get for it," Ellerbee said.

"Social Security pays them benefits," May said, picking up their quarrel again the next day. "Social Security pays up to the time the kids are eighteen years old, and they give to the widow, too. Who do you think you are, anyway? We lose a house and have to move into one not half as good because it's all we can afford, and you want to keep on paying the salaries not only of two people who no longer work for you, but to pay them out of a business that you mean to sell! Let Social Security handle it."

Ellerbee, who had looked into it, answered May. "Harold started with me this year. Social Security pays according to what you've put into the system. Dorothy won't get three hundred a month, May. And George's girl is twenty. Evelyn won't even get that much."

"Idealist," May said. "Martyr."

"Leave off, will you, May? I'm responsible. I'm under an obligation."

"Responsible, under an obligation!"

"Indirectly. God damn it, yes. Indirectly. They worked for me, didn't they? It's a combat zone down there. I should have had security guards around the clock."

5

"Where are you going to get all this money? We've had financial reverses. You're selling the store. Where's this money coming from to support three families?"

"We'll get it."

"*We'll* get it? There's no we'll about it, Mister. *You'll*. The stocks are in joint tenancy. You can't touch them, and I'm not signing a thing. Not a penny comes out of my mouth or off my back."

"All right, May," Ellerbee said. "I'll get it."

In fact Ellerbee had a buyer in mind—a syndicate that specialized in buying up businesses in decaying neighborhoods—liquor and drugstores, small groceries—and then put in ex-convicts as personnel, Green Berets from Vietnam, off-duty policemen, experts in the martial arts. Once the word was out, no one ever attempted to rob these places. The syndicate hiked the price of each item at least 20 percent—and got it. Ellerbee was fascinated and appalled by their strongarm tactics. Indeed, he more than a little suspected that it was the syndicate itself which had been robbing him—all three times his store had been held up he had not been in it—to inspire him to sell, perhaps.

"We read about your trouble in the paper," Mr. Davis, the lawyer for the syndicate, had told him on the occasion of his first robbery. The thieves had gotten away with $300 and there was a four-line notice on the inside pages. "Terrible," he said, "terrible. A fine old neighborhood like this one. And it's the same all over America today. Everywhere it's the same story. Even in Kansas, even in Utah. They shoot you with bullets, they take your property. Terrible. The people I represent have the know-how to run businesses like yours in the spoiled neighborhoods." And then he had been offered a ridiculous price for his store and stock. Of course he turned it down. When he was robbed a second time, the lawyer didn't even bother to come in person. "Terrible. Terrible," he said. "Whoever said lightning doesn't strike twice in the same place was talking through his hat. I'm authorized to offer you ten thousand less than I did the last time." Ellerbee hung up on him.

Now, after his clerks had been shot, it was Ellerbee who called the lawyer. "Awful," the lawyer said. "Outrageous. A merchant shouldn't have to sit still for such things in a democracy."

They gave him even less than the insurance people had given him for his underappraised home. Ellerbee accepted, but decided it was time he at least hint to Davis that he knew what was going on. "I'm selling," he said, "because I don't want anyone else to die."

"Wonderful," Davis said, "wonderful. There should be more Americans like you."

He deposited the money he got from the syndicate in a separate account so that his wife would

7

have no claims on it and now, while he had no business to go to, he was able to spend more time in the hospital visiting Harold.

"How's Hal today, Mrs. Register?" he asked when he came into the room where the mindless quadraplegic was being cared for. Dorothy Register was a red-haired young woman in her early twenties. Ellerbee felt so terrible about what had happened, so guilty, that he had difficulty talking to her. He knew it would be impossible to visit Harold if he was going to run into his wife when he did so. It was for this reason, too, that he sent the checks rather than drop them off at the apartment, much as he wanted to see Hal's young son, Harold, Jr., in order to reassure the child that there was still a man around to take care of the boy and his young mother.

"Oh, Mr. Ellerbee," the woman wept. Harold seemed to smile at them through his brain damage.

"Please, Mrs. Register," said Ellerbee, "Harold shouldn't see you like this."

"Him? He doesn't understand a thing. You don't understand a thing, do you?" she said, turning on her husband sharply. When she made a move to poke at his eyes with a fork he didn't even blink. "Oh, Mr. Ellerbee," she said, turning away from her husband, "that's not the man I married. It's awful, but I don't feel anything for him. The only reason I come is that the doctors say I cheer him up. Though I can't see how. He smiles that way at his bedpan."

"Please, Mrs. Register," Ellerbee said softly. "You've got to be strong. There's little Hal."

"I know," she moaned, "I know." She wiped the tears from her eyes and sniffed and tossed her hair in a funny little way she had which Ellerbee found appealing. "I'm sorry," she said. "You've been very kind. I don't know what I would have done, what *we* would have done. I can't even thank you," she said helplessly.

"Oh don't think about it, there's no need," Ellerbee said quickly. "I'm not doing any more for you than I am for George Lesefario's widow." It was not a boast. Ellerbee had mentioned the older woman because he didn't want Mrs. Register to feel compromised. "It's company policy when these things happen," he said gruffly.

Dorothy Register nodded. "I heard," she said, "that you sold your store."

He hastened to reassure her. "Oh now listen," Ellerbee said, "you mustn't give that a thought. The checks will continue. I'm getting another store. In a very lovely neighborhood. Near where we used to live before our house burned down."

"Really?"

"Oh yes. I should be hearing about my loan any time now. I'll probably be in the new place before the month is out. Well," he said, "speaking of which, I'd better get going. There are some fixtures I'm supposed to look at at the Wine and Spirits Mart." He waved to Harold.

"Mr. Ellerbee?"

"Mrs. Register?"

The tall redhead came close to him and put her hands on his shoulders. She made that funny little gesture with her hair again and Ellerbee almost died. She was about his own height and leaned forward and kissed him on the mouth. Her fingernails grazed the back of his neck. Tears came to Ellerbee's eyes and he turned away from her gently. He hoped she hadn't seen the small lump in his trousers. He said goodbye with his back to her.

The loan went through. The new store, as Ellerbee had said, was in one of the finest neighborhoods in the city. In a small shopping mall, it was flanked by a good bookstore and a fine French restaurant. The Ellerbees had often eaten there before their house burned to the ground. There was an art cinema, a florist, and elegant haberdashers and dress shops. The liquor store, called High Spirits, a name Ellerbee decided to keep after he bought the place, stocked, in addition to the usual gins, Scotches, bourbons, vodkas, and blends, some really superior wines, and Ellerbee was forced to become something of an expert in oenology. He listened to his customers—doctors

10

and lawyers, most of them—and in this way was able to pick up a good deal.

The business flourished—doing so well that after only his second month in the new location he no longer felt obliged to stay open on Sundays —though his promise to his clerks' families, which he kept, prevented him from making the inroads into his extravagant debt that he would have liked. Mrs. Register began to come to the store to collect the weekly checks personally. "I thought I'd save you the stamp," she said each time. Though he enjoyed seeing her—she looked rather like one of those splendid wives of the successful doctors who shopped there—he thought he should discourage this. He made it clear to her that he would be sending the checks.

Then she came and said that it was foolish, his continuing to pay her husband's salary, that at least he ought to let her do something to earn it. She saw that the suggestion made him uncomfortable and clarified what she meant.

"Oh no," she said, "all I meant was that you ought to hire me. I was a hostess once. For that matter I could wait on trade."

"Well, I've plenty of help, Mrs. Register. Really. As I may have told you, I've kept on all the people who used to work for Anderson." Anderson was the man from whom he'd bought High Spirits.

11

"It's not as though you'd be hiring additional help. I'm costing you the money anyway."

It would have been pleasant to have the woman around, but Ellerbee nervously held his ground. "At a time like this," he said, "you ought to be with the boy."

"You're quite a guy," she said. It was the last time they saw each other. A few months later, while he was examining his bank statements, he realized that she had not been cashing his checks. He called her at once.

"I can't," she said. "I'm young. I'm strong." He remembered her fierce embrace in her husband's hospital room. "There's no reason for you to continue to send me those checks. I have a good job now. I can't accept them any longer." It was the last time they spoke.

And then he learned that George's widow was ill. He heard about it indirectly. One of his best customers—a psychiatrist—was beeped on the emergency Medi-Call he carried in his jacket, and asked for change to use Ellerbee's pay phone.

"That's not necessary, Doc," Ellerbee said, "use the phone behind my counter."

"Very kind," the psychiatrist said, and came back of the counter. He dialed his service. "Doctor Potter. What have you got for me, Nancy? What? She did *what?* Just a minute, let me get a pencil.—Bill?" Ellerbee handed him a pencil.

12

"Lesefario, right. I've got that. Give me the surgeon's number. Right. Thanks, Nancy."

"Excuse me, Doctor," Ellerbee said. "I hadn't meant to listen, but Lesefario, that's an unusual name. I know an Evelyn Lesefario."

"That's the one," said the medical man. "Oh," he said, "you're *that* Ellerbee. Well, she's been very depressed. She just tried to kill herself by eating a mile of dental floss."

"I hope she dies," his wife said.

"*May!*" said Ellerbee, shocked.

"It's what she wants, isn't it? I hope she gets what she wants."

"That's harsh, May."

"Yes? Harsh? You see how much good your checks did her? And another thing, how could she afford a high-priced man like Potter on what *you* were paying her?"

He went to visit the woman during her postoperative convalescence, and she introduced him to her sister, her twin she said, though the two women looked nothing alike and the twin seemed to be in her seventies, a good dozen years older than Mrs. Lesefario. "This is Mr. Ellerbee that my husband died protecting his liquor store from the niggers."

"Oh yes?" Mrs. Lesefario's sister said. "Very pleased. I heard so much about you."

"Look what she brought me," Mrs. Lesefario said, pointing to a large brown paper sack.

"Evelyn, don't. You'll strain your stitches. I'll show him." She opened the sack and took out a five-pound bag of sugar.

"Five pounds of sugar," the melancholic woman said.

"You don't come empty-handed to a sick person," her sister said.

"She got it at Kroger's on special. Ninety-nine cents with the coupon," the manic-depressive said gloomily. "She says if I don't like it I can get peach halves."

Ellerbee, who did not want to flaunt his own gift in front of her sister, quietly put the dressing gown, still wrapped, on her tray table. He stayed for another half hour, and rose to go.

"Wait," Mrs. Lesefario said. "Nice try but not so fast."

"I'm sorry?" Ellerbee said.

"The ribbon."

"Ribbon?"

"On the fancy box. The ribbon, the string."

"Oh, your stitches. Sorry. I'll get it."

"I'm a would-be suicide," she said. "I tried it once, I could try it again. You don't bring dangerous ribbon to a desperate, unhappy woman."

In fact Mrs. Lesefario did die. Not of suicide, but of a low-grade infection she had picked up in the hospital and which festered along her

14

stitches, undermining them, burning through them, opening her body like a package.

The Ellerbees were in the clear financially, but his wife's reactions to Ellerbee's efforts to provide for his clerks' families had soured their relationship. She had discovered Ellerbee's private account and accused him of dreadful things. He reminded her that it had been she who had insisted he would have to get the money for the women's support himself—that their joint tenancy was not to be disturbed. She ignored his arguments and accused him further. Ellerbee loved May and did what he could to placate her.

"How about a trip to Phoenix?" he suggested that spring. "The store's doing well and I have complete confidence in Kroll. What about it, May? You like Phoenix, and we haven't seen the folks in almost a year."

"Phoenix," she scoffed, "the *folks*. The way you coddle them. Any other grown man would be ashamed."

"They raised me, May."

"They raised you. Terrific. They aren't even your real parents. They only adopted you."

"They're the only parents I ever knew. They took me out of the Home when I was an infant."

"Look, you want to go to Phoenix, go. Take money out of your secret accounts and go."

"Please, May. There's no secret account. When Mrs. Lesefario died I transferred everything back into joint. Come on, sweetheart, you're awfully goddamn hard on me."

"Well," she said, drawing the word out. The tone was one she had used as a bride, and although Ellerbee had not often heard it since, it melted him. It was her signal of sudden conciliation, cute surrender, and he held out his arms and they embraced. They went off to the bedroom together.

"You know," May said afterwards, "it *would* be good to run out to Phoenix for a bit. Are you sure the help can manage?"

"Oh, sure, May, absolutely. They're a firstrate bunch." He spoke more forcefully than he felt, not because he lacked confidence in his employees, but because he was still disturbed by an image he had had during climax. Momentarily, fleetingly, he had imagined Mrs. Register beneath him.

In the store he was giving last-minute instructions to Kroll, the man who would be his manager during their vacation in Phoenix.

"I think the Californias," Ellerbee was saying. "Some of them beat several of even the more immodest French. Let's do a promotion of a few of the better Californias. What do you think?"

"They're a very competitive group of wines," Kroll said. "I think I'm in basic agreement."

Just then three men walked into the shop.

"Say," one called from the doorway, "you got

16

something like a Closed sign I could hang in the door here?" Ellerbee stared at him. "Well you don't have to look at me as if I was nuts," the man said. "Lots of merchants keep them around. In case they get a sudden toothache or something they can whip out to the dentist. All right, if you ain't you ain't."

"I want," the second man said, coming up to the counter where Ellerbee stood with his manager, "to see your register receipts."

"What is this?" Kroll demanded.

"No, don't," Ellerbee said to Kroll. "Don't resist." He glanced toward the third man to see if he was the one holding the gun, but the man appeared merely to be browsing the bins of Scotch in the back. Evidently he hadn't even heard the first man, and clearly he could not have heard the second. Conceivably he could have been a customer. "Where's your gun?" Ellerbee asked the man at the counter.

"Oh gee," the man said, "I almost forgot. You got so many things to think about during a stickup—the traffic flow, the timing, who stands where—you sometimes forget the basics. Here," he said, "here's my gun, in your kisser," and he took an immense handgun from his pocket and pointed it at Ellerbee's face.

Out of the corner of his eye Ellerbee saw Kroll's hands fly up. It was so blatant a gesture Ellerbee thought his manager might be trying to attract the customer's attention. If that was his idea it had worked, for the third man had turned away from the bins and was watching the activity at the counter. "Look," Ellerbee said, "I don't want anybody hurt."

"What's he say?" said the man at the door who was also holding a pistol now.

"He don't want nobody hurt," the man at the counter said.

"Sure," said the man at the door, "it's costing him a fortune paying all them salaries to the widows. He's a good businessman all right."

"A better one than you," the man at the counter said to his confederate sharply. "He knows how to keep his mouth shut."

Why, they're white, Ellerbee thought. They're *white* men! He felt oddly justified and wished May were there to see.

"The register receipts," the man at the counter coaxed. Ellerbee's cash register kept a running total on what had been taken in. "Just punch Total Tab," the man instructed Kroll. "Let's see what we got." Kroll looked at Ellerbee and Ellerbee nodded. The man reached forward and tore off the tape. He whistled. "Nice little place you got here," he said.

"What'd we get? What'd we get?" the man at the door shouted.

Ellerbee cleared his throat. "Do you want to

18

lock the door?" he asked. "So no one else comes in?" He glanced toward the third man.

"What, and have you kick the alarm while we're fucking around trying to figure which key opens the place?" said the man at the door. "You're cute, you're a cutie. What'd we get? Let's see." He joined the man at the counter. "Holy smoke! Jackpot City! We're into four figures here." In his excitement he did a foolish thing. He set his revolver down on top of the appetizer table. It lay on the tins of caviar and smoked oysters, the imported cheeses and roasted peanuts. The third man was no more than four feet from the gun, and though Ellerbee saw that the man had caught the robber's mistake and that by taking one step toward the table he could have picked up the pistol and perhaps foiled the robbery, he made no move. Perhaps he's one of them, Ellerbee thought, or maybe he just doesn't want to get involved. Ellerbee couldn't remember ever having seen him. (By now, of course, he recognized all his repeat customers.) He still didn't know if he were a confederate or just an innocent bystander, but Ellerbee had had enough of violence and hoped that if he *were* a customer he wouldn't try anything dumb. He felt no animus toward the man at all. Kroll's face, however, was all scorn and loathing.

"Let's get to work," the man said who had

first read the tape, and then to Kroll and Ellerbee, "Back up there. Go stand by the aperitifs."

The third man fell silently into step beside Ellerbee.

"Listen," Ellerbee explained as gently as he could, "you won't find that much cash in the drawer. A lot of our business is Master Charge. We take personal checks."

"Don't worry," the man said who had set his gun down (and who had taken it up again). "We know about the checks. We got a guy we can sell them to for—what is it, Ron, seventeen cents on the dollar?"

"Fourteen, and why don't you shut your mouth, will you? You want to jeopardize these people? What do you make it?"

Ellerbee went along with his sentiments. He wished the bigmouth would just take the money and not say anything more.

"Oh, jeopardize," the man said. "How jeopardized can you get? These people are way past jeopardized. About six hundred in cash, a fraction in checks. The rest is all credit card paper."

"Take it," Ron said.

"You won't be able to do anything with the charge slips," Kroll said.

"Oh yeah?" Ron's cohort said. "This is modern times, fellow. We got a way we launder Master Charge, BankAmericard, all of it."

Ron shook his head and Ellerbee glanced angrily at his manager.

The whole thing couldn't have taken four minutes. Ron's partner took a fifth of Chivas and a bottle of Lafitte '47. He's a doctor, Ellerbee thought.

"You got a bag?"

"A bag?" Ellerbee said.

"A bag, a paper bag, a doggy bag for the boodle."

"Behind the counter," Ellerbee said hopelessly.

The partner put the cash and the bottle of Chivas into one bag and handed it to Ron, and the wine, checks, and credit charges into a second bag which he held on to himself. They turned to go. They looked exactly like two satisfied customers. They were almost at the door when Ron's partner nudged Ron. "Oh, yeah," Ron said, and turned back to look at them. "My friend, Jay Ladlehaus, is right," he said, "you know too much."

Ellerbee heard two distinct shots before he fell.

When he came to, the third man was bending over him. "You're not hurt," Ellerbee said.

"Me? No."

The pain was terrific, diffuse, but fiercer than anything he had ever felt. He saw himself cov-

21

ered with blood. "Where's Kroll? The other man, my manager?"

"Kroll's all right."

"He is?"

"'There, right beside you."

He tried to look. They must have blasted Ellerbee's throat away, half his spinal column. It was impossible for him to move his head. "I can't see him," he moaned.

"Kroll's fine." The man cradled Ellerbee's shoulders and neck and shifted him slightly. "There. See?" Kroll's eyes were shut. Oddly, both were blackened. He had fallen in such a way that he seemed to lie on both his arms, retracted behind him into the small of his back like a yogi. His mouth was open and his tongue floated in blood like meat in soup. A slight man, he seemed strangely bloated, and one shin, exposed to Ellerbee's vision where the trouser leg was hiked up above his sock, was discolored as thundercloud.

The man gently set Ellerbee down again. "Call an ambulance," Ellerbee wheezed through his broken throat.

"No, no. Kroll's fine."

"He's not conscious." It was as if his words were being mashed through the tines of a fork.

"He'll be all right. Kroll's fine."

"Then for *me*. Call one for *me*."

"It's too late for you," the man said.

"For Christ's sake, will you!" Ellerbee gasped. "I can't move. You could have grabbed that hoodlum's gun when he set it down. All right, you were scared, but some of this is your fault. You didn't lift a finger. At least call an ambulance."

"But you're dead," he said gently. "Kroll will recover. You passed away when you said 'move.'"

"Are you crazy? What are you talking about?"

"Do you feel pain?"

"What?"

"Pain. You don't feel any, do you?" Ellerbee stared at him. "Do you?"

He didn't. His pain was gone. "Who are you?" Ellerbee said.

"I'm an angel of death," the angel of death said.

"You're—"

"An angel of death."

Somehow he had left his body. He could see it lying next to Kroll's. "I'm dead? But if I'm dead—you mean there's really an afterlife?"

"Oh boy," the angel of death said.

They went to Heaven.

Ellerbee couldn't have said how they got there or how long it took, though he had the impression that time had passed, and distance.

It was rather like a journey in films—a series of quick cuts, of montage. He was probably dreaming, he thought.

"It's what they all think," the angel of death said, "that they're dreaming. But that isn't so."

"I could have dreamed you said that," Ellerbee said, "that you read my mind."

"Yes."

"I could be dreaming all of it, the holdup, everything."

The angel of death looked at him.

"Hobgoblin . . . I could . . ." Ellerbee's voice—if it was a voice—trailed off.

"Look," the angel of death said, "I talk too much. I sound like a cabbie with an out-of-town fare. It's an occupational hazard."

"What?"

"*What?* Pride. The proprietary air. Showing off death like a booster. Thanatopography. 'If you look to your left you'll see where . . . Julius Caesar de dum de dum . . . Shakespeare da da da . . . And dead ahead our Father Adam heigh ho—' The tall buildings and the four-star sights. All that Baedeker reality of plaque place and high history. The Fields of Homer and the Plains of Myth. Where whosis got locked in a star and all the Agriculture of the Periodic Table—the South Forty of the Universe, where Hydrogen first bloomed, where Lithium, Berylium, Zirconium, Niobium. Where Lead failed and Argon came a cropper. The furrows of gold, Bismuth's orchards. . . . Still think you're dreaming?"

"No."

"Why not?"

"The language."

"Just so," the angel of death said. "When you were alive you had a vocabulary of perhaps seventeen or eighteen hundred words. Who am I?"

"An eschatological angel," Ellerbee said shyly.

"One hundred percent," the angel of death said. "Why do we do that?"

"To heighten perception," Ellerbee said, and shuddered.

The angel of death nodded and said nothing more.

When they were close enough to make out the outlines of Heaven, the angel left him and Ellerbee, not questioning this, went on alone. From this distance it looked to Ellerbee rather like a theme park, but what struck him most forcibly was that it did not seem—for Heaven— very large.

He traveled as he would on Earth, distance familiar again, volume, mass, and dimension restored, ordinary. (*Quotidian*, Ellerbee thought.) Indeed, now that he was convinced of his death, nothing seemed particularly strange. If anything, it was all a little familiar. He began to miss May. She would have learned of his death by this time. Difficult as the last year had been, they had loved each other. It had been a good marriage. He regretted again that they had been unable to have children. Children—they would be teenagers now—would have been a comfort to his widow. She still had her looks. Perhaps she would remarry. He did not want her to be lonely.

He continued toward Heaven and now, only blocks away, he was able to perceive it in detail. It looked more like a theme park than ever. It was enclosed behind a high milky fence, the uprights smooth and round as the poles in subway trains. Beyond the fence were golden streets, a mixed architecture of minaret-spiked mosques, great cathedrals, the rounded domes of classical synagogues, tall pagodas like holy vertebrae, white frame churches with their beautiful steeples, even what Ellerbee took to be a storefront church. There were many mansions. But where were the people?

Just as he was wondering about this he heard the sound of a gorgeous chorus. It was making a joyful noise. "Oh dem golden slippers," the chorus sang, "Oh dem golden slippers." It's the Heavenly Choir, Ellerbee thought. They've actually got a Heavenly Choir. He went toward the fence and put his hands on the smooth posts and peered through into Heaven. He heard laughter and caught a glimpse of the running heels of

26

children just disappearing around the corner of a golden street. They all wore shoes.

Ellerbee walked along the fence for about a mile and came to gates made out of pearl. The Pearly Gates, he thought. There are actually Pearly Gates. An old man in a long white beard sat behind them, a key attached to a sort of cinch that went about his waist.

"Saint Peter?" Ellerbee ventured. The old man turned his shining countenance upon him. "Saint Peter," Ellerbee said again, "I'm Ellerbee."

"I'm Saint Peter," Saint Peter said.

"Gosh," Ellerbee said, "I can't get over it. It's all true."

"What is?"

"Everything. Heaven. The streets of gold, the Pearly Gates. You. Your key. The Heavenly Choir. The climate."

A soft breeze came up from inside Heaven and Ellerbee sniffed something wonderful in the perfect air. He looked toward the venerable old man.

"Ambrosia," the Saint said.

"There's actually ambrosia," Ellerbee said.

"You know," Saint Peter said, "you never get tired of it, you never even get used to it. He does that to whet our appetite."

"You eat in Heaven?"

"We eat manna."

"There's actually manna," Ellerbee said. An angel floated by on a fleecy cloud playing a harp. Ellerbee shook his head. He had never heard anything so beautiful. "Heaven is everything they say it is," he said.

"It's paradise," Saint Peter said.

Then Ellerbee saw an affecting sight. Nearby, husbands were reunited with wives, mothers with their small babes, daddies with their sons, brothers with sisters—all the intricate blood loyalties and enlisted loves. He understood all the relationships without being told—his heightened perception. What was most moving, however, were the old people, related or not, some just lifelong friends, people who had lived together or known one another much the greater part of their lives and then had lost each other. It was immensely touching to Ellerbee to see them gaze fondly into one another's eyes and then to watch them reach out and touch the patient, ancient faces, wrinkled and even withered but, Ellerbee could tell, unchanged in the loving eyes of the adoring beholder. If there were tears they were tears of joy, tears that melded inextricably with tender laughter. There was rejoicing, there were Hosannas, there was dancing in the golden streets. "It's wonderful," Ellerbee muttered to himself. He didn't know where to look first. He would be staring at the beautiful flowing raiments of the angels—There are actually raiments, he thought,

28

there are actually angels—so fine, he imagined, to the touch that just the caress of the cloth must have produced exquisite sensations not matched by anything in life, when something else would strike him. The perfectly proportioned angels' wings like discrete Gothic windows, the beautiful halos—There are actually halos—like golden quoits, or, in the distance, the lovely green pastures, delicious as fairway—all the perfectly banked turns of Heaven's geography. He saw philosophers deep in conversation. He saw kings and heroes. It was astonishing to him, like going to an exclusive restaurant one has only read about in columns and spotting, even at first glance, the celebrities one has read about, relaxed, passing the time of day, out in the open, up-front and sharing their high-echelon lives.

"This is for keeps?" he asked Saint Peter. "I mean it goes on like this?"

"World without end," Saint Peter said.

"Where's . . ."

"That's all right, say His name."

"God?" Ellerbee whispered.

Saint Peter looked around. "I don't see Him just . . . Oh, wait. *There!*" Ellerbee turned where the old Saint was pointing. He shaded his eyes. "There's no need," Saint Peter said.

"But the aura, the light."

"Let it shine."

He took his hand away fearfully and the light

29

spilled into his eyes like soothing unguents. God was on His throne in the green pastures, Christ at His right Hand. To Ellerbee it looked like a picture taken at a summit conference.

"He's beautiful. I've never . . . It's ecstasy."

"And you're seeing Him from a pretty good distance. You should talk to Him sometime."

"People can talk to Him?"

"Certainly. He loves us."

There were tears in Ellerbee's eyes. He wished May no harm, but wanted her with him to see it all. "It's wonderful."

"We like it," Saint Peter said.

"Oh, I do too," Ellerbee said. "I'm going to be very happy here."

"Go to Hell," Saint Peter said beatifically.

Hell was the ultimate inner city. Its stinking sulfurous streets were unsafe. Everywhere Ellerbee looked he saw atrocities. Pointless, profitless muggings were commonplace; joyless rape that punished its victims and offered no relief to the perpetrator. Everything was contagious, cancer as common as a cold, plague the quotidian. There was stomachache, headache, toothache, earache. There was angina and indigestion and painful third-degree burning itch. Nerves like a hideous body hair grew long enough to trip over and lay raw and exposed as live wires or shoelaces that had come undone.

There was no handsomeness, no beauty, no one walked upright, no one had good posture. There was nothing to look at—although it was impossible to shut one's eyes—except the tumbled kaleidoscope variations of warted deformity. This was one reason, Ellerbee supposed, that there was so little conversation in Hell. No one could stand to look at anyone else long enough. Occasionally two or three—lost souls? gargoyles? devils? demons?—of the damned, jumping about in the heat first on one foot then the other, would manage to stand with their backs to each other and perhaps get out a few words—a foul whining. But even this was rare and when it happened that a sufferer had the attention of a fellow sufferer he could howl out only a half-dozen or so words before breaking off in a piercing scream.

Ellerbee, constantly nauseated, eternally in pain, forever befouling himself, longed to find something to do, however tedious or make-work or awful. For a time he made paths through the smoldering cinders, but he had no tools and had to use his bare feet, moving the cinders to one side as a boy shuffles through fallen leaves hunting something lost. It was too painful. Then he thought he would make channels for the vomit and excrement and blood. It was too disgusting. He shouted for others to join him in work details —"Break up the fights, pile up the scabs"— and even ministered to the less aggravated wounds, using

31

his hands to wipe away the gangrenous drool
since there was no fabric in Hell, all clothing con-
sumed within minutes of arrival, flesh alone in-
consumable, glowing and burning with his bones
slow as phosphor. Calling out, suggesting in
screams which may have been incoherent, all
manner of pointless, arbitrary arrangements—
that they organize the damned, that they count
them. Demanding that their howls be synchro-
nous.

No one stopped him. No one seemed to be
in charge. He saw, that is, no Devil, no Arch-
fiend. There were demons with cloven feet and
scaly tails, with horns and pitchforks—They actually have horns, Ellerbee thought, there are actually pitchforks—but these seemed to have no
more authority than he had himself, and when
they were piqued to wrath by their own torment
the jabs they made at the human damned with
their sharp arsenal were no more painful—and
no less—than anything else down there.

Then Ellerbee felt he understood something
terrible—that the abortive rapes and fights and
muggings were simply a refinement of his own
attempts to socialize. They did it to make contact, to be friendly.

He was free to wander the vast burning
meadows of Hell and to scale its fiery hills—and
for many years he did—but it was much the same
all over. What he was actually looking for was

its Source, Hell's bright engine room, its storm-tossed bridge. It had no engine room, there was no bridge, its energy, all its dreadful combustion coming perhaps from the cumulative, collective agony of the inmates. Nothing could be done.

He was distracted, as he was sure they all were—"Been to Heaven?" he'd managed to gasp to an old man whose back was on fire and the man had nodded—by his memory of Paradise, his long-distance glimpse of God. It was unbearable to think of Heaven in his present condition, his memory of that spectacular place poisoned by the discrepancy between the exaltation of the angels and the plight of the damned. It was the old story of the disappointment of rising expectations. Still, without his bidding, thoughts of Paradise force-fed themselves almost constantly into his skull. They induced sadness, rage.

He remembered the impression he'd had of celebrity when he'd stood looking in at Heaven from beyond the Pearly Gates, and he thought to look out for the historic bad men, the celebrated damned, but either they were kept in a part of Hell he had not yet seen or their sufferings had made them unrecognizable. If there were great men in Hell he did not see them and, curiously, no one ever boasted of his terrible deeds or notoriety. Indeed, except for the outbursts of violence, most of the damned behaved, considering their state, in a respectable fashion, even an exemplary one. Perhaps, Ellerbee thought, it was because they had not yet abandoned hope. (There was actually a sign: "Abandon Hope, All Ye Who Enter Here." Ellerbee had read it.)

For several years he waited for May, for as long, that is, as he could remember her. Constant pain and perpetual despair chipped away at most of the memories he had of his life. It was possible to recall who and what he had been, but that was as fruitless as any other enterprise in the dark region. Ultimately, like everything else, it worked against him—Hell's fine print. It was best to forget. And that worked against him too.

He took the advice written above Hellgate. He abandoned hope, and with it memory, pity, pride, his projects, the sense he had of injustice —for a little while driving off, along with his sense of identity, even his broken recollection of glory. It was probably what they—whoever they were—wanted. Let them have it. Let them have the straight lines of their trade wind, trade route, through street, thrown stone vengeance. Let them have everything. Their pastels back and their blues and their greens, the recollection of gratified thirst, and the transient comfort of a sandwich and beer that had hit the spot, all the retrospective of good weather, a good night's sleep, a good joke, a good tune, a good time, the entire mosaic of small satisfactions that made up a life. Let them have his image of his parents

34

and friends, the fading portrait of May he couldn't quite shake, the pleasure he'd had from work, from his body. Let them have all of it, his measly joy, his scrapbook past, his hope, too.

Which left only pure pain, the grand vocabulary they had given him to appreciate it, to discriminate and parse among the exquisite lesions and scored flesh and violated synapses, among the insulted nerves, joints, muscle and tissue, all the boiled kindling points of torment and the body's grief. That was all he was now, staggering Hiroshima'd flesh—a vessel of nausea, a pail of pain.

He continued thus for several years, his amnesia willed—There's Free Will, Ellerbee thought —shuffling Hell in his rote aphasia, his stripped self a sealed environment of indifference. There were years he did not think the name Ellerbee.

And even *that* did not assuage the panic of his burning theater'd, air raid warning'd, red alert afterlife. (And that was what they wanted, and he knew it, wanting as much as they did for him to persist in his tornado watch condition, fleeing with others through the crimped, cramped streets of mazy, refugee Hell, dragging his disaster-poster avatar like a wounded leg.) He existed like one plugged into superb equipment, interminably terminal—and changed his mind and tried it the other way again, taking back all he had surrendered, Hell's Indian giver, and dredged up from where he had left them the imperfect memories of his former self. (May he saw as she had once been, his breastless, awkward, shapeless childhood sweetheart.) And when that didn't work either—he gave it a few years—he went back to the other way, and then back again, shifting, quickly tiring of each tack as soon as he had taken it, changing fitfully, a man in bed in a hot, airless room rolling position, aggressively altering the surfaces of his pillow. If he hoped—which he came to do whenever he reverted to Ellerbee —it was to go mad, but there was no madness in Hell—the terrific vocabulary of the damned, their poet's knack for rightly naming everything which was the fail-safe of Reason—and he could find peace nowhere.

He had been there sixty-two years, three generations, older now as a dead man than he had been as a living one. Sixty-two years of nightless days and dayless nights, of aggravated pain and cumulative grief, of escalated desperation, of not getting used to it, to any of it. Sixty-two years Hell's greenhorn, sixty-two years eluding the muggers and evading the rapists, all the joyless joy riders out for a night on his town, steering clear of the wild, stampeding, horizontal avalanche of the damned. And then, spinning out of the path of a charging, burning, screaming inmate, he accidentally backed into the smoldering ruin of a second. Ellerbee leaped away as their bodies touched.

"Ellerbee?"

Who? Ellerbee thought wildly. Who?

"Ellerbee?" the voice repeated.

How? Ellerbee wondered. How can he know me? In this form, how I look . . .

Ellerbee peered closely into the tormented face. It was one of the men who had held him up, not the one who had shot him but his accomplice, his murderer's accomplice. "Ladlehaus?" It was Ellerbee's vocabulary which had recognized him, for his face had changed almost completely in the sixty-two years, just as Ellerbee's had, just as it was Ladlehaus's vocabulary which had recognized Ellerbee.

"It is Ellerbee, isn't it?" the man said.

Ellerbee nodded and the man tried to smile, stretching his wounds, the scars which seamed his face, and breaking the knitting flesh, lined, caked as stool, braided as bowel.

"I died," he said, "of natural causes." Ellerbee stared at him. "Of leukemia, stroke, Hodgkin's disease, arteriosclerosis. I was blind the last thirteen years of my life. But I was almost a hundred. I lived to a ripe old age. I was in a Home eighteen years. Still in Minneapolis."

"I suppose," Ellerbee said, "you recall how *I* died."

37

"I do," Ladlehaus said. "Ron dropped you with one shot. That reminds me," he said. "You had a beautiful wife. May, right? I saw her photograph in the Minneapolis papers after the incident. There was tremendous coverage. There was a TV clip on the Six O'clock News. They interviewed her. She was—" Ellerbee started to run. "Hey," the accomplice called after him. "Hey, wait."

He ran through the steamy corridors of the Underworld, plunging into Hell's white core, the brightest blazes, Temperature's moving parts. The pain was excruciating, but he knew that it was probably the only way he would shake Ladlehaus so he kept running. And then, exhausted, he came out the other side into an area like shoreline, burning surf. He waded through the flames lapping about his ankles and then, humiliated by fatigue and pain, he did something he had never done before.

He lay down in the fire. He lay down in the slimy excrement and noxious puddles, in the loose evidence of their spilled terror. A few damned souls paused to stare at him, their bad breath dropping over him like an awful steam. Their scabbed faces leaned down toward him, their poisoned blood leaking on him from imperfectly sealed wounds, their baked, hideous visages like blooms in nightmare. It was terrible. He turned over, turned face down in the shallow river of pus and shit. Someone shook him. He didn't move. A man straddled and penetrated him. He didn't move. His attacker groaned. "I can't," he panted, "I can't—I can't see myself in his *blisters*." That's why they do it, Ellerbee thought. The man grunted and dismounted and spat upon him. His fiery spittle burned into an open sore on Ellerbee's neck. He didn't move. "He's dead," the man howled. "I think he's dead. His blisters have gone out!"

He felt a pitchfork rake his back, then turn in the wound it had made as if the demon were trying to pry foreign matter from it.

"Did he die?" Ellerbee heard.

He had Free Will. He wouldn't move.

"Is he dead?"

"How did he do it?"

Hundreds pressed in on him, their collective stench like the swamps of men dead in earthquake, trench warfare—though Ellerbee knew that for all his vocabulary there were no proper analogies in Hell, only the mildest approximations. If he didn't move they would go away. He didn't move.

A pitchfork caught him under the armpit and turned him over.

"He's dead. I think so. I think he's dead."

"No. It can't be."

"I think."

"How? How did he do it?"

"Pull his cock. See."

"No. Make one of the women. If he isn't dead maybe he'll respond."

An ancient harridan stooped down and rubbed him between her palms. It was the first time he had been touched there by a woman in sixty-two years. He had Free Will, he had Free Will. But beneath her hot hands his penis began to smoke.

"Oh God," he screamed. "Leave me alone. Please," he begged. They gazed down at him like teammates over a fallen player.

"Faker," one hissed.

"Shirker," said another scornfully.

"He's not dead," a third cried. "I told you."

"There's no death here."

"World without end," said another.

"Get up," demanded someone else. "Run. Run through Hell. Flee your pain. Keep busy."

They started to lift him. "Let go," Ellerbee shouted. He rolled away from a demon poking at him with a pitchfork. He was on his hands and knees in Hell. Still on all fours he began to push himself up. He was on his knees.

"Looks like he's praying," said the one who had told him to run.

"No."

"Looks like it. I think so."

"How? What for?"

And he started to pray.

"Lord God of Ambush and Unconditional Surrender," he prayed. "Power Play God of Judo Leverage. Grand Guignol, Martial Artist—"

The others shrieked, backed away from him, cordoning Ellerbee off like a disaster area. Ellerbee, caught up, ignoring them, not even hearing them, continued his prayer.

"Browbeater," he prayed, "Bouncer Being, Boss of Bullies—this is Your servant, Ellerbee, sixty-two-year fetus in Eternity, tot, toddler, babe in Hell. Can You hear me? I know You exist because I saw You, avuncular in Your green pastures like an old man on a picnic. The angeled minarets I saw, the gold streets and marble temples and all the flashy summer palace architecture, all the gorgeous glory locked in Receivership, Your zoned Heaven in Holy Escrow. The miracle props—harps and Saints and popes at tea. All of it—Your manna, Your ambrosia, Your Heavenly Host in their summer whites. So can You *hear* me, pick out my voice from all the others in this din bin? Come on, come on, Old Terrorist, God the Father, God the Godfather! The conventional wisdom is we can talk to You, that You love us, that—"

"I can hear you."

A great awed whine rose from the damned, moans, sharp cries. It was as if Ellerbee alone had not heard. He continued his prayer.

"I hear you," God repeated.

41

Ellerbee stopped.

God spoke. His voice was pitchless, almost without timbre, almost bland. "What do you want, Ellerbee?"

Confused, Ellerbee forgot the point of his prayer. He looked at the others who were quiet now, perfectly still for once. Only the snap of localized fire could be heard. God was waiting. The damned watched Ellerbee fearfully. Hell burned beneath his knees. "An explanation," Ellerbee said.

"For openers," God roared, "I made the heavens and the earth! Were you there when I laid the foundations of the firmament? When I—"

Splinters of burning bone, incandescent as filament, glowed in the gouged places along Ellerbee's legs and knees where divots of his flesh had flared and fallen away. "An *explanation*," he cried out, "an *explanation!* None of this what-was-I-doing-when-You-pissed-the-oceans stuff, where I was when You colored the nigger and ignited Hell. I wasn't around when You elected the affinities. I wasn't there when You shaped shit and fashioned cancer. Were *You* there when I loved my neighbor as myself? When I never stole or bore false witness? I don't say when I never killed but when I never even raised a hand or pointed a finger in anger? Where were You when

I picked up checks and popped for drinks all round? When I shelled out for charity and voted Yes on the bond issues? So no Job job, no nature in tooth and claw, please. An explanation!"

"You stayed open on the Sabbath!" God thundered.

"I what?"

"You stayed open on the Sabbath. When you were just getting started in your new location."

"You mean because I opened my store on Sundays? That's why?"

"You took My name in vain."

"I took . . ."

"That's right, that's right. You wanted an explanation, I'll give you an explanation. You wanted I/Thou, I'll give you I/Thou. You took It in vain. When your wife was nagging you because you wanted to keep those widows on the payroll. She mocked you when you said you were under an obligation and you said, 'Indirectly. G–d damn it, yes. Indirectly.' 'Come on, sweetheart,' you said, 'you're awfully g–ddamn hard on me.'"

"That's why I'm in Hell? *That's* why?"

"And what about the time you coveted your neighbor's wife? You had a big boner."

"I coveted no one, I was never unfaithful, I practically chased that woman away."

"You didn't honor your father and mother."

Ellerbee was stunned. "I did. I *always* honored my father and mother. I loved them very much. Just before I was killed we were planning a trip to Phoenix to see them."

"Oh, *them*. They only adopted you. I'm talking about your natural parents."

"I was in a Home. I was an *infant*!"

"Sure, sure," God said.

"And *that's* why? *That's* why?"

"You went dancing. You wore zippers in your pants and drove automobiles. You smoked cigarettes and sold the demon rum."

"These are Your reasons? *This* is Your explanation?"

"*You thought Heaven looked like a theme park!*"

Ellerbee shook his head. Could this be happening? This pettiness signaled across the universe? But anything could happen, everything could, and Ellerbee began again to pray. "Lord," he prayed, "Heavenly Father, Dear God—maybe whatever is is right, and maybe whatever is is right isn't, but I've been around now, walking up and down in it, and *ev*erything is true. There is nothing that is not true. The philosopher's best idea and the conventional wisdom, too. So I am praying to You now in all humility, asking Your forgiveness and to grant one prayer."

"What is it?" God asked.

Ellerbee heard a strange noise and looked around. The damned, too, were on their knees—

all the lost souls, all the gargoyles, all the demons, kneeling in fire, capitulate through Hell like a great ring of the conquered.

"What is it?" He asked.

"To kill us, to end Hell, to close the camp."

"Amen," said Ellerbee and all the damned in a single voice.

"Ha!" God scoffed and lighted up Hell's blazes like the surface of a star. Then God cursed and abused Ellerbee, and Ellerbee wouldn't have had it any other way. *He*'d damned him, no surrogate in Saint's clothing but the real Mc-Coy Son of a Bitch God Whose memory Ellerbee would treasure and eternally repudiate forever, happily ever after, world without end.

But everything was true, even the conventional wisdom, perhaps especially the conventional wisdom—that which had made up Heaven like a shot in the dark and imagined into reality halos and Hell, gargoyles, gates of pearl, and the Pearl of Great Price, that had invented the horns of demons and cleft their feet and conceived angels riding clouds like cowboys on horseback, their harps at their sides like goofy guitars. Everything. Everything was. The self and what you did to protect it, learning the house odds, playing it safe —the honorable percentage baseball of existence.

Forever was a long time. Eternity was. He would seek out Ladlehaus, his murderer's accomplice, let bygones be bygones. They would

45

get close to each other, close as family, closer. There was much to discuss in their fine new vocabularies. They would speak of Minneapolis, swap tales of the Twin Cities. They would talk of Ron, of others in the syndicate. And Ladlehaus had seen May, had caught her in what Ellerbee hoped was her grief on the Six O'clock News. They would get close. And one day he would look for himself in Ladlehaus's glowing blisters.

Part II **THE BOTTOM LINE**

adlehaus was chewing the fat with Ellerbee, reminiscing about his days as an accomplice and accessory.

"You used to be a handbag?" Ellerbee said.

"A handb—? Oh yeah. You know I never used to get jokes? I could tell them once I heard them, I had a good ear, but I never understood why folks laughed. That's interesting, too," he said. "If a fellow told a joke I thought it was a true story. I never laughed at punch lines. It was only when other folks were around and I heard them laugh that I knew."

"'Folks'?" Ellerbee said. "A hotshot accomplice like you says 'folks'?"

"Death softens the tongue," Ladlehaus said, "it kindly's us." He barely recognized himself in Ellerbee's blisters. "I've aged," he said.

"You were aged to begin with," Ellerbee said. "All right," he said, "let me." He combed Ladlehaus's back for a reflection. They were like apes grooming each other.

"It's how I got into crime in the first place," Ladlehaus said, turning around, "not getting the point of jokes, I mean."

Ellerbee said, "Don't squirm. I know what you mean. When you didn't laugh they thought you were tough. They perceived as character what was only affliction. They hard-guy'd you, they street corner'd and candy stored you. I *know* what you mean."

"They scaffolded my body with switchblades and pieces," Ladlehaus said.

"I *know* what you mean."

"They Saturday night special'd me. 'We can get Ladlehaus,' they'd say. But *so* tough in their imaginations that at first they wouldn't risk it."

"Trigger-happy. I *know* what you mean. We can only exchange information. Then what happened?"

"The usual."

"The usual? I didn't move in your circles. I don't know what you mean. What was the usual in your circles?"

"They put me behind steering wheels with

52

my headlamps off and my motor running a half block upwind from the scenes of crimes."

"Oh yes."

"It was progress of a sort, training. Everybody gets better at things, everybody gets the big break. Opportunity knocks. I never had a record. Did I tell you? I had no record."

"You told me."

"I lived to be almost a hundred and died of natural causes—an organic, unbleached death like something brought back from the Health Food Store. And no record." He looked at his friend, at his cooked face, reduced as ember. "You know," he said, "this is very decent of you, Ellerbee. In your position I'm not sure I wouldn't harbor a grudge."

"It's too hot to harbor a grudge," Ellerbee said.

"It's ironic," Ladlehaus said dreamily, "I was an accomplice to your murder and now we're good pals."

"It's too hot to be good pals," Ellerbee said, and ran off howling.

God came to Hell. He was very impressive, Ladlehaus thought. He'd seen Him once before, from a distance—a Being in spotless raiment who sat on a magnificent golden throne. He looked different now. He was clean-shaven and stood before Ladlehaus and the others in a carefully tailored summer suit like a pediatrician in a small town, a smart tie mounted at His throat like a dagger. The flawless linen, light in color as an army field cot, made a quiet statement. He was hatless and seemed immensely comfortable and at ease. Ladlehaus couldn't judge His age.

"Hi," God said. "I'm the Lord. Hot enough for you?" He asked whimsically and frowned at the forced laughter of the damned. "Relax," He said, "it's not what you think. This isn't a harrowing of Hell, there'll be no gleaning or winnowing. I'm God, not Hodge. It's only an assembly. How you making out? Are there any questions?" God looked around but there were no takers. "No?" He continued, "where are My rebels and organizers, My hotshot bizarrerie, all you eggs in one basket curse-God-and-diers? Where are you? You—punks, Beelzebubs, My iambic angels in free fall, what's doing? There are no free falls, eh? Well, you're right, and it's okay if you don't have questions.

"The only reason I'm here is for ubiquitous training. I'm Himself Himself and I don't know how I do it. I don't even remember making this place. There must have been a need for it because everything fits together and I've always been a form-follows-function sort of God, but sometimes even I get confused about the details. Omniscience gives Me eyestrain. I'll let you in on something. I wear contacts. Oh yes. I grind the lenses Myself. They're very strong. Well, you can imagine.

You'd go blind just trying them on. And omnipotence—*that* takes it out of you. I mean if you want to work up a sweat try omnipotence for a few seconds. To heck with your jogging and isometrics and crash diets. Answering prayer—that's another one. Plugged in like the only switchboard operator in the world. You should hear some of the crap I have to listen to. 'Dear God, put a wave in my hair, I'll make You novenas for a month of Sundays.' 'Do an earthquake in Paris, Lord, I'll build a thousand-bed hospital.'

"You like this? You like this sort of thing? Backstage with God? Jehovah's Hollywood? Yes? Or maybe you're archeologically inclined? Historically bent, metaphysically. Well here I am. Here I am that I am. God in a good mood. Numero Uno Mover moved. Come on, what would you *really* like to know? How I researched the Netherlands? Where I get My ideas?"

"Sir, is there Life before Death?" one of the damned near Ladlehaus called out.

"What's that," God said, "graffiti?"

"Is there Life before Death?" the fellow repeated.

"Who's that? That an old-timer? Is it? Someone here so long his memory's burned out on him, his engrams charred and gone all ashes? Can't remember whether breakfast really happened or's only part of the collective unconscious?

How you doing, old-timer? Ladlehaus, right?"

Ladlehaus remained motionless, motionless, that is, as possible in his steamy circumstances, in his smoldering body like a building watched by firemen. He made imperceptible shifts, the floor of Hell like some tightrope where he juggled his weight, redistributing invisible tensions in measured increments of shuffle along his joints and nerves. All he wanted was to lie low in this place where no one could lie low, where even the disciplined reflexes of martyrs and stylites twitched like thrown dice. And all he could hope was that pain itself—which had never saved anyone—might serve him now, permitting him to appear like everyone else, swaying in place like lovers in dance halls beneath Big Bands.

"You, Ladlehaus!" the Big Band leader blared.

Throughout the Underworld the nine thousand, six hundred and forty-three Ladlehauses who had died since the beginning of time, not excepting the accomplice to Ellerbee's murder, looked up, acknowledged their presence in thirty tongues. These are my family, Ladlehaus thought, and glanced in the direction of the three or four he could actually see. Their blackened forms, lathered with smoke and fire damage, were as meaningless to him, as devoid of kinship, as the dry flinders of ancient bone in museum display cases. Meanwhile God was still out there. "Not *you*," He said petulantly to the others, "the *old*-timer."

He means *me*, Ladlehaus thought, this shaved and showered squire God in His summer linens means *me*. He means *me*, this commissioned officer Lord with his myrrh and frankincense colognes and aromatics and His Body tingling with morning dip and agency, all the prevailing moods of fettle and immortality. He means *me*, and even though he knew there had been a mistake, that he'd not been the one who'd sounded off, Ladlehaus held his tongue. He means me, He makes mistakes.

"So you're the fellow who spouts graffiti to God, are you?" God said and Ladlehaus was kneeling beneath Him, hocus-pocus'd through Hell, terrified and clonic below God's rhetorical attention. "Go," God said. "Be off." And Ladlehaus's quiet "Yes" was as inaudible to the damned as God's under-the-breath "Oops" when He realized His mistake.

And Ladlehaus thought Well, why not? He didn't know me any better when He sent me here. He didn't know my heart. I was an accomplice, what's that? No hit man, no munitions or electronics expert sent from far, no big deal Indy wheel-man and certainly no mastermind. Only an accomplice, a lookout, a man by the door, like a sentry or a commissionaire, say, little

more than an eyewitness really. Almost a mascot.
And paid accordingly, his always the lowest share,
sometimes nothing more than a good dinner and
a night on the town. The crimes would have
taken place without him. An accomplice, a red-
cap, a skycap, a shuffler of suitcases, of doggy
bags of boodle, someone with a station wagon,
seats that folded down to accommodate cartons
of TV sets, stereos. What was the outrage? Even
the business of his having been an accomplice to
Ellerbee's murder, though true, was as much talk
as anything else, something to give him cachet in
his buddy's eyes, an assertion that he'd left a
mark on a pal's life. And God said "Be off," and
he was off.

The first thing he was aware of was the darkness. A blow of blackness—speleological. He was
somewhere secret, somewhere doused. Not void
but void's quenched wilderness. All null subfusc
gloom's bleak eclipse. Hell was downtown by
comparison—unless this was Hell too, some lead-
lined, heavy-curtained outpost of it. (And Ladlehaus afraid of the dark.) Was it still the universe?

And then he recalled his heresy—He makes
mistakes—and thought he knew. He hasn't been
here, He never made this. And thought: Nihility.
I am undone. And had to laugh because he knew
he was right this time. Why, I'm dead, he thought,

I'm the only dead man. Hadn't he, hadn't all of
them, been snatched from life to Hell? He thought
of cemeteries. (Why didn't he know where he
was buried? Because he had not been dead, not
properly dead.) Of survivors with their little flags
and wreaths and flowers, their pebbles laid like
calling cards on the tops of tombstones. No one
was ever there, that's why they thought they had
to leave their homeopathic evidences on the
graves of their loved ones, why they barbered
those graves and, stooping, plucked out weeds,
overgrowth, fluffing up the ivy over bald spots
in the perpetual care. But the loved ones would
never know, they weren't dead, only gone to Hell.
(He means *me*, Ladlehaus thought, He's quick
to anger and He makes mistakes and I'm the only
dead man. And Ladlehaus as afraid of death as
of darkness because wasn't it strange that for all
his sojourn in Hell he could not recall a moment
of real fear?) It was funny, all those Sunday
vigils at graveside, solemn funerals and even the
children well turned out, sober and spiffy, to say
a ceremonial goodbye to a being already fled, the
body in the coffin only an illusion, and a lousy
illusion at that. (He'd seen his share of open
caskets, the Tussaud effigies actually redolent of
wax.) "But no one's *here*," he wanted to shout.
"Until today there *were* no dead. We are not a
pasty people. We're brindled, varnished as violins
and cellos, rusted as bloodstain."

He missed his pain. Settled as stone, fixed as laminate souvenir or gilded baby shoe, Ladlehaus mourned his root-canal'd nerves, insentient now as string. There was not even phantom pain, the mnemonic liveliness of amputated limbs, and if this was at first a comfort—Ha ha, Ladlehaus thought—it was now, he saw—Ha ha, Ladlehaus thought—the ultimate damnation. People were right to fear the dark, death. It was better in land-mined Hell where one had to watch one's step, where reflex family'd the damned to mountain goats—We were the Goats of Hell, Ladlehaus thought, proud of the designation as the suede and leathered weekend vicious—leaping puddles of boobytrap, learning the falls. Almost conceited. Not because of the attention but because of immortality in such disaster circumstances. Not survival or endurance but the simple inability to stop the steeplechase, to be forced to run forever in jeopardous double time the spited sites of the Underworld, punished in its holocaustal climate and periled along its San Andreas fallibilities, stubbing his toes on the terrible rimmed blossoms of its buried volcanos, eternally tenured in its hurricane alleys and tidal wave bays. In life he had known the Alcatraz'd and Leavenworth'd, all the Big Housed, up-the-river'd chain-gang incarcerate. Like himself they had fattened on sheer grudge, but what was their grudge to his own, to that of the infant damned and the riteless stricken? Temper had tempered him and made him what he had never been as a man, made him, that is, dangerous, lending his very body outrage and turning him into a sort of torch, a *real* accomplice now to the five-alarm arson of Hell, firing its landscape and using it up with his pain. Which he missed. Because it had kept him company. (What had his friendship with Ellerbee amounted to? Three encounters? Four? Perhaps eighteen or nineteen minutes all told in all the years he'd been in the Underworld. Hell's measly coffee break.)

Now there was just—He makes mistakes, what did He think He was proving?—lonely painless Ladlehaus, his consciousness locked into his remains like a cry in a doll. (For he felt that that was where he was, somewhere inside his own remains, casketed, coffin'd, pine boxed, in his best suit, the blue wool, the white button-down, the green tie pale as lettuce. But bleached now certainly and in all probability decomposed, the fabric returned not to fiber but to compost, mixed perhaps with his flesh itself so that his duds wore him, an ashen soup, and Ladlehaus only a sort of oil spill tramping his own old beach like a savage footprint. Though this didn't bother him. He had broken the habit of his body long ago, since old age, before, disabused of flesh, separated from it as from active service.) But it was so dark, dark as pupil, darker.

"I used to be Jay Ladlehaus." He paused. "Who did you used to be?" There was no answer. "So this is death," he said. "Well I'm disappointed. It's very boring. Where I come from—I come from Hell—it wasn't ever boring. There was always plenty to do. There was fire, panic in the streets, looting weather. You should have heard us. All those Coconut Grove arias. Our yowls and aiees like the scales of terror. The earthquakes and aftershocks. We could have been holidaymakers, folks ripped out of time on weekends in night-clubs, families in bleachers collapsing on Bat Day. Titanicized, Lusitania'd, Hindenburg'd, Pompeii'd. And very little grace under pressure down there, forget your women and children first protocols, your Alfonse and Gastonics. Men were men, I tell you. Men were men, poor devils.

"Well— So what's happening? Where's the action? When? Or is it all monologue here? It's enough to make you laugh—the way they bury us, I mean. Obsequies and exequies. Cortege and kist. Limousines and hearses—death's dark motor pool. Oh boy. You'd think a government had changed hands. Well— So what do the rest of you Ken and Barbie dolls think? What's the bottom line, eh?"

"Oatcakes."

"Oatcakes?" said astonished Ladlehaus. "Oatcakes is the bottom line?"

"Oatcakes! Oatcakes!"

(There had been darkness but not silence. He'd been distraught, nervous. Well sure, he thought, you get nervous in new circumstances —your first day in kindergarten, your grave. Now he listened, hearing what had been suppressed by his anguish and soliloquies. It was a soft and mushy sound, gassy. Amplified it could have been the noise of chemical reactions, of molecules binding, the caducean spiral of doubled helices or the attenuated pop of parthenogenesis like the delicate withdrawal of a lover. It might have been the sound of maggots burrowing or cells touching at some interface of membrane, the hiss of mathematics.)

"Hello?" Ladlehaus called. "Sir?" ("Be off," God had said.) He saw a way out. If he could just get the fellow's attention— "I'm Jay Ladlehaus," he shouted, "and through a grievous error I've been buried alive. Inadvertently interred. There wasn't any foul play, you needn't be alarmed. *You* couldn't get in trouble. 'Honor bright.' We say 'Honor bright' in our family when the truth's involved and we take a holy oath. You got a shovel?"

"Oatcakes," Quiz said.

So, Ladlehaus thought gloomily, it's my incorporeality. No more voice than a giraffe. And settled down with his thoughts for eternity with not even pain left to stimulate him. Not seeing how he could make it and wishing that God had closed down his consciousness too. "Well it isn't picturesque," he said. His hope had been for a peaceful afterlife, something valetudinarian, terminally recuperative, like his last years in the Home perhaps, routinized, doing the small, limited exercises of the old, leaving him with his two bits worth of choice, asking of death's nurses that his pillows be fluffed, his bed raised inches or lowered, and on nice mornings taking the sun, watching game shows on television in the common room, kibitzing bridge, hooked rugs, the occupational therapies, the innocuous teases and flirtations of the privileged doomed. And hearing the marvelous gossip of his powerless fellows, his own ego—though he'd never been big in that line —sedated, sedate, nival, taking an interest in the wily characters of others, in their visitors and their visitors' calm embarrassments. He could have made an afterlife of that, not even arrogating to himself wisdom, some avuncular status of elder statesman, content to while away the centuries and millennia as, well, a sort of ghost. It would have been, on a diminishing scale, like hearing the news on the radio, reading the papers. A sort of ghost indeed. Dybbuk'd into other peoples' lives, their gripes and confidences a sort of popular music. What could be better? Death like an endless haircut. "Forget it, Ladlehaus," he said, "forget it, old fellow." And resigned himself in what he continued to think of as a cemetery, a wide, deep barracks of death.

Later—it might have been minutes, it could have been days—he heard the voice again. "Oatcakes," it said, diminished this time, softened, and Ladlehaus tried again, his heart not in it.

"Excuse me," he said, "I have been inadvertently interred. Dig where the stone says 'Ladlehaus.' He was my cousin. We were very close."

Quiz heard him. He had heard him yesterday when he had come to eat his lunch on the bench near Ladlehaus's stone and had discovered that Irene had packed oatcakes for him. Quiz had recently been told by his doctor that he had excessively high blood pressure, hypertension, and, in addition to his diuretics, had been commanded to go on a strict low-fat, low-salt, sugar-free diet. He had been told that he must eat natural foods only.

He did not terribly mind the restriction of sweets and seasonings, but he found the health foods extremely distasteful. Unnatural, if you asked him. The sunflower cakes and shrimp-flavored rice wafers, the infinite soybean variations tricked out in the consistency of meats, the greens and queer vegetables, their odd shapes and colors like mock-ups of the private parts of flowers. The little pudding cups of honey with their garnish of wheat germ and lecithin. "He can live a normal life," the doctor told Irene. "I *live* a normal life," Quiz had said. "Your pressure's dangerously elevated," the doctor said. "Irene, tell him. Am I hypertense?" "He's cool as a cucumber, Doctor. He don't ever brood or get angry." "Trust me, Mrs. Quiz," the doctor said, "Mr. Quiz's triglycerides are off the charts and he has engine room pressure. If you want him around you'll have to put him on the diet." "Ain't that stuff expensive?" "What's your life worth to you, Mr. Quiz?" So he went obediently on the diet.

So he had heard the fellow Ladlehaus. Buried alive. Inadvertently interred. Did Ladlehaus think he was a fool? There were his dates plain as day right there on his tombstone. Dead eleven years. Now how did the fellow expect him to believe a cock-and-bull story like that? Quiz was no spooney. Locked in the ground eleven years and still alive? Impossible. Not worth the bother of a reply really.

Quiz finished his lunch, wiped bits of oatcake from the corner of his mouth with a napkin. Silly, he thought. Lips like a horse's. Then the diuretics took effect. He'd read that the human body was about 70 percent water. If he kept getting the urge his would be a lot less than that in no time. "I'll be landlocked, a Sahara of a man." He stood up but saw that he was going to be caught short. Hurriedly the groundskeeper un-zipped and relieved himself.

"Can you hear me?" Ladlehaus asked. "There's been a terrible mistake. If you'd just get a shovel, sir. Or come back with your mates. Can you hear me?"

Of course Quiz heard him. I've got high blood pressure, he wanted to say, I'm not deaf. But he held his tongue, wouldn't give Ladlehaus the satisfaction, insulting his intelligence like that. He was only a groundskeeper in the new high school's stadium, Quiz knew, no genius certainly, but no damn fool either. That was one of the things that got the passively hypertense grounds-keeper down. Everybody was always trying to fool you, tell you a tale, make you believe things that weren't so. Politicians with *their* promises, the military, the papers, the gorgeous commer-cials on television. A fellow worked hard and scraped just to keep body and soul together, and right away he was a target for the first man who came along with something to sell. Sometimes, when you didn't know, you had to go along. Now he might have high blood and he might not and it just wasn't worth it to him to defy the doctor to find out. But when even the dead lied to you that was something else. That was some-thing he could do something about. He told Irene.

"There's this dead man near the bleachers," he said. "Fellow named Ladlehaus."

"Oh? Yes?"

"Keeps nagging at me with a cock-and-bull story about being buried alive. Wants me to dig him out. Calls me 'sir,' and wants to know do I have a shovel. Dead as a doornail but you should hear some of the stuff he comes up with. I give him high marks for invention."

"Just ignore him," Irene said, "don't let him upset you. Tell him you've got high blood, engine room pressure. Tell him your triglycerides are off the charts and he should leave you alone."

"Wouldn't give him the satisfaction," Quiz said.

"That's how to deal with him," the wife agreed.

"Insulting my intelligence."

"Called it a name, did he?"

"But I fixed him," Quiz confided.

"How's that, my darling?"

"I peed on him."

Through a kind of sortilege, Ladlehaus's was the only grave allowed to remain where it was when the city fathers closed down the new section of the municipal cemetery under its right of eminent domain. They picked the site for the new high school after several feasibility studies had been made. Ladlehaus would have been surprised to learn that he lay between the track and the bleachers-like grandstand in a plot of consecrated ground no larger than a child's bedroom. He would have been astonished to learn that for a time there had been serious talk of naming the new school in his honor. A feasibility study was made. He had no record so that was in his favor, and he had outlived everyone whom he had ever served as an accomplice. The difficulty was that he had no surviving relatives to speak up for him, and the people in the Home whose gossip and small talk had been the comfort of his last years either did not remember him at all or recalled his appreciative silences and attention as the symptoms of a man far gone in senility. The upshot was that the school was named for the contractor who had purchased the honor with a kickback to the chairman of the committee which had done all the feasibility studies. Thus it was that Nick Capiapo High School had gained its name and was not called after a man who had not only had actual conversation with God and who had the distinction, like a player of Monopoly who gets a "Bank Error in Your Favor" card, of receiving the courtesy of His holy "Oops," but who was the only man in the long sad history of time ever to die.

Reassured by his wife that he had taken the right course with Ladlehaus, Quiz now regularly ate his lunch near Ladlehaus's grave, hoping the organic scents of honey and fiber, of phallic vegetable and subtropical fruit, of queer nuts heavily milligramed with potent doses of Recommended Daily Allowance, fetid to his own meat-and-potatoes temperament, might prove actually emetic to the dead man's. For the caretaker, who was neither drawn to nor repudiated the living, hated Ladlehaus and took an active dislike to this decomposing horror beneath the grassy knoll at the bleachers' bottom. He acknowledged the unreason of his aversion.

"Maybe," he told Mrs. Quiz, "it goes deeper than his trying out his ghost tricks on me. I'd treat him the same if he was a genie in a bottle. These dead folks have got to be stopped, Irene."

"Don't let him bother you. You must concentrate on cleaning up your lipids, on scraping the last pre-digested enzymes off your plate. Don't let him get your goat, my lover."

"Him? Bother me? That ain't the way of it by half. I been teasing him, drawing him in, having him on. I make out there's a war right here in St. Paul."

"Here? In the Twin Cities?"

"*Between* the Twin Cities."

"Stand at ease, men. Smoke if you got 'em. That a comedy book you got in your fatigues, Wilson? No, I don't want to see it. Put it in your pack. Renquist, leave off reading that letter from your sweetheart or you'll wear it out. All right.

Now the captain wanted me to talk to you about the meaning of this war. He wants you to know what you're fighting for, and do you understand the underlying geopolitical reasons and whatnot. Well, I'll tell you what you're fighting for. So's the bastards don't sweep down from Minneapolis and do their will on our St. Paul women. So's they don't wreak their wicked ways on our children. Let me tell you something, gentlemen. A St. Paul baby ain't got no business on the point of a Minneapolis bayonet. You seen for yourselves on Eyewitness News at Ten what happened after Duluth signed the surrender papers with them. Looting, rape, the whole shooting match. Them Duluth idiots thought they could appease the enemy's blood lust. Well, you seen how far *that* got 'em. So it's no time to be reading comical books, and if you birds ever hope to see peace with honor again you better be prepared to fight for it.

"Whee-herr-whee-herr-whee-herr!

"There's the air-raid warning, boys. Capiapo, you and your men take cover. You, Phillips, your squad's in charge of Hill Twelve.

"Hrr-hrr. Hrn. Hrn-hrn.

"It don't need no fixed bayonets, Sarge. Dey's *our* tanks. Ain' dat so, Gen'rul?

"It *is*, Mr. President."

History had gone out of whack, current events had run amok. Ladlehaus despaired. Hear-

ing what he did not know were Quiz's master
sergeants and the high blood-pressured man's
High Command, his presidents and sirens and
generals and tanks, he accepted in death what
he had not known in Hell—that the great issues
which curdled and dominated one's times were
shorter-lived and more flexible than personality
or character. In his own lifetime he had outlived
depressions and dictators, wars and the peace
that came between them, outlived the race questions and the religious, all the great ideas and
great men who thought them, outlasting the
trends and celebrated causes. What he wanted to
know was what Wilson thought of his comic
book, what Renquist's sweetheart had to say.

"Is there anything bothering you, Mr. Quiz?"
the caretaker's doctor asked him. "Mrs. Quiz tells
me that you've been sticking to your diet and
taking your medications, yet your pressure's as
high as it ever was. Are you under any particular
stress at work?"

"Some dead man's been trying to play me for
a sucker."

"Hsst," Ladlehaus said. "Hsst, Renquist."

"He's trying to get to me through my men,"
Quiz told his wife.

* * *

"Boys," Quiz asked the ten- and eleven-year-olds who had the Board of Education's permission to use the facilities of the high school stadium, "do you know what a dirty old man is?"

They made the jokes Quiz had expected them to make when he asked his question, and Quiz smiled patiently at their labored gags and misinformation. "No, boys," he said when they had done, "a dirty old man is none of those things. Properly speaking, he's very sick. For one reason or another his normal sexual needs—do you know what normal sexual needs are, boys?—have not been met and"—he waited for their raucous miniature laughter and hooting to die down—"he has to take his satisfaction in other ways. It's much the same as hunger. Now I doubt if any of you boys has ever really been hungry, but let's suppose that your mom never lets you have candy. Let's suppose you never chew gum or drink soda, that she doesn't let you eat ice cream or nibble peanuts. That you can't have fruit. The only sweets she lets you have are vegetables—corn, say, or sweet potato, sugar beets, squash." He waited for them to mouth the false "yechs" and mime the fake disgust he knew they would mouth and knew they would mime.

"What might happen in such a case, boys, is that you'd grow up with a sick sweet tooth. You wouldn't know what to do with *real* candy. A Hershey's might kill you, you could drown in a Coke.

"It's the same with dirty old men, boys. Maybe they can't have a relationship—do you know what a relationship is, boys?—with a person their own age, so they seek out children. Your moms are right, boys, when they tell you not to accept rides from strangers, to take their nickels or share their candy. Children are vulnerable, children. They don't know the score. You give a dirty old man an inch he'll take a mile. His dick will be in your hair, boys, he'll put your wiener in his pocket. They can't help themselves, boys, but dirty old men do terrible things. They want to smell your tush while it's still wet, they want to heft your ballies and blow up your nose. They want to ream and suck, touch and diddle. They want to eat your poo-poo, boys."

He had their attention.

"Do you know why I say these things to you?"

They couldn't guess.

"Because I'm thirty-seven years old, boys. Raise your hands if your daddies are older than me." Nine of the twenty children raised their hands. "See?" Quiz said, "almost half of you have pops older than I am. They're not old. *I'm* not old.

"The other thing I wanted to say, boys, is that I have a *good* relationship with Irene. Irene

74

is my wife. We do it three times a week, boys. There's nothing Irene won't do for me, boys, and I mean *nothing*." He listed the things Irene would do for him. "Do you know why I tell you these things, boys?"

They couldn't guess.

"To show I can have a relationship with a person my own age. To show I'm not dirty. I'm not old, I'm not dirty.

"So that when I tell you what I'm going to tell you you'll know it isn't just to get you to come over to the grandstand with me."

The attack had started. Ladlehaus could hear the foot soldiers—their steps too indistinct for men on horseback—running about in the death-grounds. From time to time he heard what could only have been a child cry out and, once, their commander. "Cover me, cover me, Flanoy," the commander commanded.

"Yes, sir, I'll cover you," the child shouted. He heard shots of a muffled crispness, reduced by the earth in which he lay to a noise not unlike a cap pistol. He held his breath in the earth, lay still in the grids of gravity that criss-crossed his casket like wires in an electric blanket.

Horrible, he thought, horrible. Attacking a cemetery. Defending it with children. A desperate situation. He had fought in France in the war. Captured three of the enemy. Who'd turned out to be fifteen-year-old boys. But these kids could not have been even that old. What could they be fighting about? He was disappointed in the living, disappointed in Minneapolis.

"Stop," Ladlehaus cried. "This is a cemetery. A man's buried here."

"How was the kohlrabi?" Irene asked.

"I dropped the kohlrabi during the charge on that wiseguy's grave."

"Kohlrabi's expensive."

"You should have heard him. What a howl."

"Regular katzenjammer, was it?"

"You think it's right, Irene? Using kids to fight a man's battles for him?"

"The kids weren't hurt," she said. "Umn," she said, "oh my," she said, squeezing his dick, hooking down and kissing it, twirling him about so she could smell his tush. "Umn. Yum yum. What's more important," she asked hoarsely, her pupils dilated, "that a few kids have bad dreams, or that my hypertense husband keel over with a stroke just because some nasty old dead man is trying to get his goat? Ooh, what have we here? I think I found the kohlrabi."

The boys didn't have bad dreams. They were ten years old, eleven, their ghosts domesticated, accepted, by wonder jaded. O.D.'d on miracle, awe slaked by all unremitting nature's *coups de*

76

théâtre, they were not blasé so much as comfortable and at ease with the thaumatological displacements of Ladlehaus's magic presence. Still he insisted on coming at them with explanations, buried alive stuff, just-happened-to-be-passing-by, to-be-in-the-neighborhood constructions, glossing the stunning marvel of his high connections with death. They knew better, it was stranger to be alive than to be dead. They could read the dates on his marker. Perhaps he'd forgotten.

And forgave him. Not grudging Ladlehaus his lies as the crazy janitor had whose hypertension—they wouldn't know this, couldn't—was merely the obversion of his ensnarement by the real. A janitor—they wouldn't know *this*—a man of nuts and bolts, of socket wrenches, oil cans, someone a plumber, someone a painter, electrician, carpenter, mechanic—trade winded, testy.

So if they dreamed it was of dirty old men, not ghosts.

"Where were you yesterday, Flanoy?" Ladlehaus asked.

"Yesterday was Sunday."

They swarmed about his grave, lay down on the low loaf of earth as if it were a pillow. Or stretched out their legs on his marker, their heads lower than their feet. They plucked at the crowded stubble of weeds, winnowing, combing, grooming his mound.

"Does it tickle or pinch when I do this?" a

boy asked and pulled a blade of grass from its sheath in Ladlehaus's grave.

"When you do what?"

For they had come through their war games, outlasted Quiz's supervision of their play, outlasted their own self-serving enterprises of toy terror and prop fright. (For a while they had dressed up in his death, taking turns being Ladlehaus, running out from beneath the grandstands, flapping their arms as if they waved daggers, making faces, screeching, doing all the tremolo vowel sounds of what they took to be the noise of death. It hadn't worked. "It's not dark enough to be scary," Muggins, the youngest boy said, and kicked the side of Ladlehaus's grave.) And settled at last into a sort of intimacy—the period when they teemed about his grave, grazing it like newborn animals at some trough of breast.

They looked up at the sky, their hands behind their heads.

"What's it like in your casket, Mr. Ladlehaus?"

"Do you sleep?"

"No."

"Are you hungry?"

"No."

"Does it smell?"

"No."

"Does it hurt?"

"Not now."

"Is it awful when it rains?"

"What's worse, the summer or the snow?"

"Are you scared?"

"Sometimes."

"Are there maggots in your mouth, Mr. Ladle-haus? Are there worms in your eye sockets?"

"I don't know. Who's that? Ryan? You're a morbid kid, Ryan."

"Shepherd."

"You're morbid, Shepherd."

"Did you ever see God?"

"Yes."

"Have you ever seen Jesus?"

"Jesus *is* God, asshole."

"Don't use that word, Miller."

"He's right, Miller. Mr. Ladlehaus has seen God. He's an angel. Don't say 'asshole' near an angel."

The boys giggled.

"Do you know the Devil?"

"I've seen the damned," Ladlehaus said softly.

"What? Speak up."

"I've seen the damned." It was curious. He was embarrassed to have come from Hell. He felt shame, as if Hell were a shabby address, something wrong-side-of-the-tracks in his history. He'd been pleased when they thought him an angel.

Quiz watched impassively from a distance.

"Be good, boys," Ladlehaus urged passionately. "Oh *do* be good."

"He's telling them tales," the caretaker reported to his wife.

"You boys get away from there," Quiz said. "That's hallowed ground."

They play in cemeteries now, he thought, and tried to imagine a world where children had to play in cemeteries—death parks. (Not until he asked was he disabused of his notion that there had actually been a war. What disturbed him—it never occurred to him, as it had never occurred to the boys, that the war was for his benefit—were his feelings when he still thought there had actually been a battle—feelings of pride in the shared victory, of justification at the punishment meted out to the invaders from Minneapolis. All these years dead, he thought, all those years in Hell, and still not burned out on his rooter's interest, still glowing his fan's supportive heart, still vulnerable his puny team spirit. All those years dead, he thought, and still human. Nothing learned, death wasted on him.)

But a world where children could play in cemeteries and nuzzle at his little tit of death. He shuddered. He who could feel nothing, less tactile than glass, his flesh and bone and blood amputated, a spirit cap-side by a loose bundle of pencils, buttons, thread, nevertheless had some- where somehow something in reserve with which to shudder, feel qualms, willies, jitter, tremor, the mind's shakes, all its disinterested, volitionless flinch. And at what? Sociology, nothing but soci- ology. Who had lived in Hell and seen God and who had, it was to be supposed, a mission. Who represented final things, ultimates, whose destiny it was to fetch bottom lines. A sentimental accom- plice, an accessory gone soft. (For he'd felt noth- ing when the bullet sang which had dropped his pal, Ellerbee, felt nothing for the people—he'd have been a teenager then—at whose muggings he'd assisted, felt nothing presiding at the empty- ing of wallets, cash drawers, pockets—he had quick hands, it was his kind of work, he was good at it —and once, on a trolley commandeered by his fellows actually belly to belly with the conductor, quickly depressing the metal whosis of the terri- fied man's change dispenser, lithely catching the coins in his free hand and rapidly transferring dimes to one pocket, quarters, nickels and pennies to others.)

But he had not gone soft. Remorse was not his line of country, no more than sociology. A question plagued him. Not why children played in cemeteries but where the officials were who permitted it. Where, he wondered, was the man who said "Oatcakes"? Or the fellow who'd led the boys in war games? He was outraged that, exiled in earth, appearances had not been kept up. He could imagine the disorder of his grave— candy wrappers, popsicle sticks, plugs of gum on his gravestone. He wanted it naked, the litter cleared. It was his fault for talking to them in the first place. He'd dummy up.

"You! Ladlehaus!"

"Hey, Ladlehaus. The kids won't come near you. I told them some garbage about hallowed ground."

"Hey you, Ladlehaus, how's your cousin?"

"That's better. That's the ticket. Silence from the dead. You leave us alone, we'll leave you alone."

"God is not mocked. He is not fooled. He is not sorrowful. He is not disappointed. He is not expectant. He is not worried. He doesn't hold His breath. He does not hope or wish upon a star. He is not waiting till next year or contemplating changes in the lineup. He is not on the edge of His seat. He is complete as spider or bear. As stone or bench he is complete.

"It is only we who are unfinished. And God is indifferent as history. He has not abandoned a world He had never embraced or set much stock in.

"Other preachers tell you to welcome God into your hearts as if He were some new kid in the neighborhood or a fourth for Bridge. What good is such advice? He will not come. He is complete. He has better things to do with His time. He doesn't accept invitations. He doesn't go out. He stays home nights. His home is Heaven. Death is His neighborhood. Life is yours.

"He asks nothing of us, beloved. Not our lives, not our hearts. He would not know what to do with such gifts. He would be embarrassed by them. He does not write Thank You notes. He is not gracious. He is not polite or conventional. He has no thought for the thought that counts.

"What would the thought count *for?*

"He is God and there is an Iron Curtain around Him. His saints are bodyguards, Secret Service.

"Why then be good? Because He will smash us if we aren't. Those are the rules.

"Let us pray.

"Our Father Who art in Heaven, we, your servants, humbly beseech Thee. Bless World Team Tennis in St. Paul.

"Amen."

"Yeah yeah, sure sure, Amen," said a voice in the ground near Ilie Nastase's feet.

*   *   *

"What's World Team Tennis?" asked the Lord on High.

"Boys? Boys? Where am I, boys?"

Quiz smiled.

"No need to whisper, Nurse. Mr. Ladlehaus is in coma. There's reason to believe they coma dream, although I doubt they can actually hear us —particularly when they're under as deep as this one is."

Ladlehaus wondered.

"Is he any better today? Let me see the chart, please. Hmn. Wait a minute, did you see this? Never mind, it's only a smudge. For a minute I thought— Hold it a moment. Look here. The way this line seems to go up. That's the sort of thing we're looking for."

Ladlehaus wondered.

"No, it's important, I'm *glad* you called. All right, let me see if that resident was right. By golly, I think he *was*. *Those* aren't smudges. Did you change machines? Right. Excellent. Quite

84

frankly I'm not prepared to say yet just *what* it means. It's too early to tell, but this is evidence, this is definitely evidence. See this trough, this spike. Pass me one of your oatcakes. This *is* exciting. Extremely so. Now if he can only be made to produce more readings like these, establish a pattern rather than these virtuoso performances, I think we might have real hope of going to them and— See to the I.V., please, Nurse. A man on the mend needs nourishment!"

Ladlehaus hoped.

"I wanted you to see these, Doctor," the woman said.

"I felt so silly," she said.
"You did just fine, Irene."

"It's hopeless. They won't accept my interpretation of the readings," Quiz said in a voice as much like his own doctor's as he could make it.
"Not? Why?"
"They say it's only an aberration, that the electrical impulses could come from his body heat, that brain death has already taken place."
"But that's so unfair, Doctor."
"She's right," Ladlehaus said. "It hasn't taken place," he said. "It *hasn't*. Get me more I.V. I hear

85

perfectly. The nurse asked why they won't accept the readings and you said they think it's an aberration. It isn't an aberration."

"They may be right of course," Quiz said, "though I hate to admit it. —Damned vultures. Death with dignity indeed! Folderol. Fiddlededee. The only reason they want to pull the plugs is to get at his fortune and power. —All those millions!"

"Don't let them," Ladlehaus screamed. "Don't let them get at my fortune and power. Oh I know you can't hear me, but look, look at the machine. I'll squeeze out my best brain waves for you. Don't let them. Those millions are mine. I earned them."

"It's a shame," the nurse said, "after all the good he's done."

"All the good, yes," Ladlehaus said, "all the millions, all the good I've done."

"Look at these, Doctor, would you? They're slightly different from the others. What do you make of them?"

"Flyspecks, I should think, scratchings of coma dream. But let me have them. Perhaps the judge will grant a stay."

Ladlehaus hoped.

"Uncle Jay, you high table, five star, Hall of Fame prick! You mashed potato! You spinach leaf! Do you recognize my voice, you bloodless fake? It's your nephew Jack—Rita's husband. And I'll tell you what I'm going to do, you cabbage! I'm going to tamper your charts and splash in your brain waves. But I'll give you a fighting chance. If you're not dead scream 'no,' or forever hold your peace."

"No! *No!*"

"So. Silence. Ashes to ashes, you salad. Just a slight adjustment of the tone arm on your electroencephalogram and— Why, Nurse, you startled me. I was just looking at my uncle's charts here."

"Sir, no one is permitted in the Intensive Care Unit unless accompanied by the patient's physician."

"I'm his nephew. I thought, seeing he's dying and all, I'd look in on him and say goodbye in private."

"No one is permitted in the Intensive Care Unit, no one. If you were Mrs. Ladlehaus herself I'd have to tell you the same thing."

"Mrs. La— The blonde bombshell? Me? That twat?"

"You'll have to leave."

"Just going, just going. So long, Unc, see you around the victory garden."

"That will be all, sir. Do I have to call an orderly?"

"Call a garbage truck."

"Orderly!"

"I'm going, I'm *going*."

"Thank you, Nurse."

Ladlehaus was hopeful.

"Well?"

"It's bad. Here."

"This is a court order."

"It's *the* court order."

"I'm sorry."

"Step in, please, Deputy. This is Deputy Evers, Nurse."

"Ma'am."

"He's here to see that we comply with the order."

"Wait!"

"Wait a moment, Doctor."

"Nurse?"

"It's just that I know your convictions about such things. Deputy Evers, this man has taken the Hippocratic oath. Pulling the plug on Mr. Ladlehaus's life support systems would be a violation of everything the doctor believes. It would go against nature and inclination, and do an injustice not only to his conscience but to his training. I can't let him do that."

"I'm sorry, ma'am, but the court or—"

"I read the court order, Deputy. I know what it says. What *I* say is that I can't let him do it."

"Look, lady—"

"I'll do it myself."

"Nurse!"

"Please, Doctor. I'm only grateful it was me on duty when the order came down. Deputy, you won't say a word about this. Not if you're a Christian."

"I don't know. The order says— Sure. Go ahead."

"Do it now, Nurse. Pull them. The man's all but dead anyway. He has only his coma dream. You pull that, too, the moment you remove those plugs."

"I hadn't thought of that."

"It's why I fought so hard to keep him on the L.S.S. But go ahead. The law's the law."

"Someone better do it," the deputy said.

"I'll do it now," said the goodhearted nurse.

"When I'm geting better?" Ladlehaus cried. *"When I can hear everything you say? When I can practically taste the iodoform in here? When I no longer dream I was ever in Hell? When I have my millions and my power? When I have my blonde bombshell?"*

"Pop," the nurse said.

And poor, dead, puzzled, grounded Ladlehaus heard their mean duet laughter and died again, and once again, and kept on dying, in their presence dying, dying beneath them, with each spike and trough of their laughter.

*   *   *

"His name is Quiz."

They were near him again, not all but some, and this time the man Quiz did not bother to shoo them off. Ladlehaus sensed arrangement, order. Not the wide barracks of death now—he knew where he was, the child had told him—but rows of folding chairs. He sensed they were chairs, had sensed it that afternoon when a disgruntled Quiz had snapped them into place in the grass, aligned them, something martial in their position- ing, discrete as reviewing stand.

Behind him he heard the gruff shuffle of men's good shoes as they sidestepped along the cement ledges of the grandstand. (He couldn't *know* this, couldn't smell the lightly perfumed faces of the women or the crisp aftershaves and colognes of the men. For him the soft rustle of the women's dresses might have been the languid swish of flags in a low wind, the brusque adjust- ments of the men's trousers like in-gulps of hushed breath.) He listened carefully, but could not make out the words of the adults.

"After the recital my daddy is taking us to Howard Johnson's. I'm going to have a coffee ice cream soda."

"Coffee ice cream keeps me up."

They're some more of his accomplices, Ladlehaus thought. They're going to take me for another ride.

Then a woman made an announcement. He listened for some quaver of theatricality in the voice that would give her away, reveal her as the "nurse" in a different role. Talk always sounded like talk, never like a speech. Something read aloud or memorized or even willfully extemporaneous could never pass for the flat, halting, intimate flow of unmanaged monologue or conversation. Even a man on the radio, scriptless, and talking apparently as he might talk among his friends in a lunchroom, sounded compromised by the weight of his thousand listeners. Even a child at prayer did. But the woman was marvelous. Ladlehaus had to admire the cast Quiz had assembled. She wanted to thank Miss Martin and Miss Boal for their generous and untiring assistance in putting together tonight's program, extending right down to helping the students tune their instruments. She mustn't forget to thank the principal, Dr. Mazlish, for opening up the facilities of the high school to the Community Association of Schools of Arts, or CASA, as it had come to be known. She particularly wanted to thank the parents for encouraging and, she supposed, at times *insisting* that the children practice their instruments. And, as coordinator for the program, now in its third year, she particularly wanted to thank the children themselves for the devotion they showed to their music and for their willingness to share their accomplishments with the good audience of parents, relatives, and friends who had come out to hear them tonight. Tonight's recital was only the first. There would be three others with different young performers during the course of the summer. She regretted that the dates for these had not yet been settled or they would have been printed on the back of the program. Speaking of the program, she said, Angela Kinds and Mark Koehler, though listed, would be unable to perform this evening. They would be rescheduled for one of the recitals later in the summer. In the event of inclement weather, she added, arrangements would be made to hold those indoors.

She was magnificent. It was perfectly obvious to Ladlehaus that she had done the whole thing working from small white note cards held discreetly in her right hand.

He had forgotten about music, forgotten harmony, the grand actuality of the reconciled. Forgotten accord and congruence—all the snug coups of correspondence. He did not remember balance. Proportion had slipped his mind and he'd forgotten that here was where the world dovetailed with self, where self tallied with sympathy and distraction alike. He had forgotten dirge and dead-march, scherzo, rondo, jig and reel. He had

92

forgotten the civilized sound of a cello, or that violins indeed sounded like the woe of gypsies. He had not remembered the guitar, lost the sound of flutes, had no recall for the stirring, percussive thump in melody—all the gay kindling points of blood, the incredible flexibility of a piano. What he had for eyes wept what he had for tears.

A child played "Lightly Row." He wept. They had Waxman's "The Puzzle," Gesanbuch's "Sun of My Soul." He wept. Bartok's "Maypole Dance" was played, Lully's Gavotte. There was Bach's Prelude in F, Chopin's Mazurka in B flat Major, Bohm's "Gypsy" and Copland's "The Cat and the Mouse." He wept for all of them. One of the advanced students—he knew they were students now; professionals would have played better, actors not as well—gave them—for it was "them" now too, the dead man subsumed with the living —Brower's Three Etudes, and Ladlehaus sighed, his moods flagrant, ventriloquized by the homeopathic instance of the music, the dead man made generous, tolerant, supportive of all life's magnificent displacements. Why, I myself am a musician, he thought, my sighs music, my small luxurious whimpers, my soul's high tempo, its brisk tattoo and call to colors. There is a God, the man who had spoken to Him thought, and murmured, "It's beautiful. The Lord is with me."

And He was. He lay over Ladlehaus's spirit like a flag on a casket.

"I was drawn by the music," God said. "I come to all the recitals. I'm going to take Dorset. I like what she did with Bach's Fantasy in C Minor."

"Hush, no talking," said the boy who had identified Quiz.

"That one too," God said more softly. "His 'Sheep May Safely Graze' made me all smarmy."

"No," Ladlehaus said.

"I give him six months," He said confidently.

"No," Ladlehaus pleaded, "it's Flanoy. Flanoy's only a child."

"Oh, please," said God, "it's not that I hate children but that I love music."

Quiz had stationed himself on the bench where he had taken his low-fat, gluten-free, ortho-molecular lunches. This was where he heard the disturbance. He rose from the bench and moved beside Ladlehaus's grave. There, in plain view of the crowd, he began to stomp on Jay Ladlehaus's marker.

"Hold it down, hold it *down*, you!"

"Quiz!" Ladlehaus shouted.

The caretaker blenched. He tried to explain to Mazlish, the principal. "He *knows*," he cried, "he knows who I am." On his knees he pounded with his fists on Ladlehaus's grave. He grabbed divots of hallowed ground, sanctified earth, and smeared them across his stone. They tried to drag him away. Quiz wrapped his arms about the dead man's marker. "What are you doing?" he screamed, "I've got hypertension. I take low-cal minerals, I'm strictly salt-free. I eat corrective lunch!"

"*Get him!*" Ladlehaus hissed. "*Get him. He's a composer!*"

And God, who knew nothing of their quarrel but owed Ladlehaus a favor, struck Quiz dead.

It would not be so bad, he thought in the momentary shock wave of silence that followed the commotion. It would not be so bad at all. He would exist in nexus to track meets, to games, to practices and graduations, and spend his death like a man in a prompter's box beneath all the ceremonies of innocence the St. Paul Board of Education could dream up, spending it as he had spent his life, accomplice to all the lives that were not his own, accessory to them, accomplice and accessory as God.

A composer, he thought, I told Him he was a composer. Well, He makes mistakes, Ladlehaus thought fondly. Ladlehaus sighed and hoped for good weather.

But he did not know that the caretaker's death had come at a point in the recital when God knew that those children who had already performed would be getting restless, beloved.

Part III

THE STATE

OF

THE ART

uiz, in Hell, was making the point that he had been slain.

"You're dead, you're a dead man, just one more goner," Lesefario said.

"No, no. My pop's a dead man, all the folks on the old man's side with their bad histories and amok blood counts—they're dead men. I was definitely slain. Smited. Blasted. Here today gone today. Slain absolutely. And none of the amenities, let me tell you, no last words or final cigarette, the blindfold unoffered. It was as if I'd gotten in to start my car and—boom! Like someone ambushed, snuffed by unions, eating in restaurants and rushed by hit men."

"Do you know who did it?"

"I've got my suspicions, I'm working on it, I have some leads. I've— Hey— Where are you going? Hey."

But Lesefario was gone, vanished in Hell's vast smoke screen, the fiery fog that was its climate.

Because it was the fate of the damned to run of course, not jog, run, their piss on fire and their shit molten, boiling sperm and their ovaries frying; what they were permitted of body sprinting at full throttle, wounded gallop, burning not fat—fat sizzled off in the first seconds, bubbled like bacon and disappeared, evaporate as steam, though the weight was still there, still with you, its frictive drag subversive as a tear in a kite— and not even muscle, which blazed like wick, but the organs themselves, the liver scorching and the heart and brains at flash point, combusting the chemistries, the irons and phosphates, the atoms and elements, conflagrating vitamin, essence, soul, yet somehow everything still within the limits if not of endurance then of existence. Damnation strictly physical, nothing personal, Hell's lawless marathon removed from character. "Sure," someone had said, "we hit the Wall with every step. It's all Wall down here. It's wall-to-wall Wall. What, did you think Hell would be like some old-time baker's oven? That all you had to do was lie down on a pan like dough, the insignificant heat bringing you out, fluffing you up

100

like bread or oatmeal cookies? You think we're birthday cake? We're fucking *stars*. Damnation is hard work, eternity lousy hours."

So if Lesefario ran it was his fate to do so, only his body's kindled imperatives. But he might have run anyway, getting as far as he could from Quiz and his crazy talk about suspicions and leads, angrier at who'd put him there than at his oiled rag presence itself, holding a grudge which in others went up faster than fat, resentment as useless in these primed, mideast circumstances as hope or apology. Also, it made Lesefario wistful, nostalgic, all that talk of slaying and snuffing. It was George's own last memory. He'd been a clerk in Ellerbee's liquor store in Minneapolis, an employee who'd worked for the younger man fifteen years, whose crimes were almost victimless, a little harmless chiseling making change and, once, the purchase of some hijacked wine at discount. Certainly nothing that would warrant the final confrontation with the stickup men who'd taken first Ellerbee's money, then his clerk's life, shooting him down for no reason, for target practice. "To teach you a lesson," his killer had said, and taught him his death. It wasn't much as these things went, but it was Lesefario's last human contact and he treasured it.

Meanwhile Quiz collared everyone he could, fixing them with the tale of his unexpected end, sudden as comeuppance.

"I make no charges," he screamed as they double-timed through fire storm in their Dresden tantrum. "I make no charges, I've got no proof, but a thing like that, all that wrath, those terrible swift sword arrangements, that's the M.O. of God Himself!"

God overheard Quiz's complaints. They were true and, briefly, surprised Him. Which also surprised Him, Who, unaccustomed to surprise, did not immediately recognize the emotion, for Whom the world and history were fixed as house odds, Who knew the grooves in phonograph records and numbered the knots in string. Which was a little silly of course. Not without truth, but silly. As though He were the Microfiche God, Lord of the Punched Cards.

That He had smote Quiz struck Him as odd, an act like an oversight. The man had been a groundskeeper in a high school stadium. God had stopped by to hear some children in a summer recital and Quiz had interrupted the performance. I overreacted, thought God, as mildly bemused as He had been briefly surprised.

Because He was no street brawler, not really, though people didn't appreciate this. He made His reputation in the old days. It was all there in the Bible. Now that was a good book, He thought. He thought. *He* thought. He does so much thinking He thought because He has no one to talk

102

to, He thought. Though We were always a good listener. Folks were constantly sending Him their prayers. Tykes in Dr. Dentons. People in churches. All the bowed-head, locker room theology of teams in contention, the invocations at rallies, the moments of silent prayer, the grace notes at a hundred billion suppertimes, all the laymen of Rotary, Elks, Shrine, and Jaycees. God, God thought, needs din, its mumbled gimme's.

And He used to listen. He had taken requests. He had smote the Egyptians, knocked off this tribe or that. Well, it was the worship. He was a sucker for worship. To this day a pilgrimage turned His heart, the legless, like athletes, pulling themselves up the steps of great cathedrals, the prostrate humble face down in dog shit.

He summoned His only begotten son, a young man in his early thirties, a solid, handsome figure who, in life, might once have had skills. He appeared in the doorway of the mansion. There was about him a peculiar, expectant attitude, alerted but ambivalent, not nervous but deferential, like a new cabinet minister standing by microphones near his president. He wore a plain but clearly expensive, loose-fitting robe cinched at the waist. A small, carefully crafted Cross with a half-nude figure not so much suspended from it as vaguely buckled to it, the back arched and the knees slightly raised, flexed as an astronaut's on his couch, hung about his throat.

The hands, pinioned to the transverse, were
nailed at the lifeline and along the forward edges
of the palms, rendering it impossible to make a
fist. The ankles were crossed, beveled, studded
with thick, crude nails.

His Father glanced without pleasure from
His only begotten son's jewelry to the hands crippled at his sides, each hand still in that same stiff
equivocal position, neither open nor shut and,
holding nothing, giving the impression that they
had once been folded and had just now been
pulled apart.

God nodded for the son to approach and
winced as the young man staggered forward in
that odd rolling gait of the lame, each sandaled
foot briefly and alternately visible beneath the
long robes as he labored toward Him, the toes
crushed, twisted, almost braided, suggesting a
satyr orthopedics, the wrongly angled, badly set
bones of the hidden legs.

"Please," God said, "sit."

The son of God paused, looked around,
spotted what he'd been looking for. "So," he said,
"You kept it."

"Of course," God said.

Jesus lowered himself onto the crude round-
less stool. It was almost a parody of furniture, a
kid's first effort in Shop, the badly turned spindles
dropsical, rough, caulked at their holes with
shim. He'll hurt himself, God thought, but the

son had the cripple's tropism, his lurching, awkward truce with gravity. "It holds me," he said.

"Yes."

"That's right," Christ said. He looked down. "I couldn't make apprentice today," he said softly.

"You did your crucifix well enough."

The son smiled. "What, this old thing?" he seemed to say. Then, in a moment, he did speak. "I raised the dead," he said. "I ran them up like flags on poles. I gave the blind 20/20 and lepers the complexions of debutantes. Miracle was my métier. This," he said, brushing the crucifix with fingers that would never be straight, "nothing to it. It was wished into being. It's a snapshot is all, a Christ's gilded baby shoe, sentimental as a lock of hair. Like it? It's True Cross by the way. But no hands made it."

"You've no forgiveness, have you? There isn't enough love in you to flesh out a song."

"The apple doesn't fall—"

"Stop that," the Father said.

"Wondering where You went wrong, Papa? Why I'm such a surly saviour? Look at it this way. These things happen in the holiest of families."

"No. You've no forgiveness."

"Me?" Christ said, "I was built to forgive. I give away dispensation like a loss leader. There isn't a horror they can dream up I don't change into cheesecake in the blink of an eye. I go to

Yankee Stadium when the home team's away and the evangelist comes and it's standing room only for the fans of salvation, and I do it there, under the lights, hitting to all fields, God's designated hitter, and it's forgive and forget and bygones be bygones. So don't tell *me* I've no forgiveness. Why, I'm made of pardon and commutation and forgiveness like the laws of bankruptcy or the statute of limitations. And why not? What did any of those poor bastards ever do to me?"

"All right," God said, "I want you to take *My* case."

"Your case?"

"I smote a man."

"You—?"

"His name was Quiz. He irritated Me. He made a disturbance during a recital and ruined My concentration. I overreacted."

"You *smote* him?"

"I already told you," the Lord said irritably. The Christ giggled. "So?" God said.

"So?"

"Do what you do to those other poor bastards. Absolve Me, shrive Me, wipe My slate. Put Me on your tab, pick up My check. Carry Me. Forgive Us Our debts as We forgive Our debtors, Luv."

Though the words were flippant, there was a sort of urgency behind them, a sense He gave off not of rage but of rage cornered, its energy turned to reason. Poor Quiz, Christ thought. "Sure," Christ said finally, "for the slaying of Quiz I forgive You."

"You never understood anything, did you?" the Lord asked murderously. "You never got into the spirit of things."

"I thought I *was* the Spirit of things," the young man said meekly.

"Lamb!" God roared.

"We were talking about Quiz."

"We were never talking about Quiz."

"No," he said softly, rising awkwardly from the stool as his Father watched. He used his body to steady himself and, turning, stamped the floor like a tap dancer, kicking at leverage, purchase, with his cripple's volitionless two-step. "I loved it there," he said. "I loved being alive."

God looked at His son thoughtfully. "Well," the Lord said, "in conversation at least you can still turn the other cheek. How's your mother?"

"Ah," said the Christ.

Quiz was making a name for himself among the damned. He never let up ranting, each day bringing his charges. It could not have been madness. Paranoia was vaporized even more swiftly than grudge. So, after a while, they began to believe him and, in spite of their own pain, even to take his side. Quiz seemed to be everywhere at once, like a celebrity in a small town.

"I was Pearl Harbor'd," he might scream, "December Seventh'd by the Lord. Is that fair? I ask you. Men die, have heart attacks, wear out. Mostly wear out. The junkman won't touch them, Detroit recall them. And, yes, I grant that some go sudden. There are accidents. Accidents happen. Mother Nature fucks up. Kids dart into traffic, balls roll in the street. But that's only physics, it's physics is all. Guys buy it in war and that's physics, too. And a crime of passion's a flexing of glands. It's physics, it's science.

"Been stung by a wasp? By hornets, crazed bees? They were doing their duty, following Law. With me it was different. God came from His hive. I was stung by the Lord!"

Then one day he was calmer, changed. "It don't hurt anymore," he announced. They looked at him curiously. "The pain, I can't feel it. It must pay to complain." He felt himself carefully, dabbing experimentally at his wounds, the steaming sores and third-degree skin. He poked his fingers in the flaming craters of his flesh, the smoking, dormant cones of erupted boils. "They've turned off the juice. Look," he said, "look." And, stooping, gathered a bolus of fire and placed it on his tongue. "See?" he said, chewing the flame, moving it about like mouthwash, snapping it like gum. "See? It ain't any more spice to it than a bite of hot dinner. I frolic in fire, I heigh-ho

108

in heat!" He played with brimstone for them, he waded in flames like a child at the shore. "I think they've decided to do something for me, I think they're afraid I might sue."

Lesefario and the others who saw him crossed themselves in the presence of the miracle, but all they got for their pains was pain, their foreheads and breasts like so many blazing crosses on so many lawns.

She was a modest woman, self-effacing, old-fashioned, downright shy. Intact. A virgin by temperament and inclination as much as compulsion or circumstance. More. Something actually spinster in her nature, a quality not of maiden since that term had about it a smell of the conditional, but of the permanently chaste. Something beyond chastity, however—chastity, in her case at least, not so much a choice as a quality, like the shade of her skin or the height she would be, fixed as her overbite. Something beyond chastity, beyond even repression.

It was one of the reasons she'd been chosen, of course. As Saint Joan had been chosen for the breadth of her shoulders, her sinewy arms. It was one of the reasons she'd been chosen, He'd reminded her, in their rare interviews. It was one of the reasons she'd been chosen. Yes. She agreed. It was the cruelest reason. To have to listen to the—to her—ironic litany, unceasing, continuous as the noise of summer. She would never get used to it, over it, the humiliation as stinging after two thousand years as the first time she'd heard it and realized it was she they meant. "Hail Mary," she heard, "full of grace, blessed art thou among women, and blessed is the fruit of thy womb, Jesus." Nice, she thought. A fine way to talk, excuse me, pray. Her most intimate parts called out as familiarly as her name, associating her with a femaleness she not only did not understand but actually repudiated, freezing her forever not just in fecundity but in a kind of sluttishness.

And for all the world she was The Virgin Mary, the capital letters and epithet like something scrawled in phone booths or spray-painted in subways. The snide oxymorons repugnant to her. Virgin Mother, Immaculate Conception. Her story known throughout the world, carried by missionaries to hinterland, boondock, clearing, sticks; parsed by savages, riddled by New Guinea stone-agers, all the bare-breasted and loinclothed who stood for whatever she could not stand, almost the first thing they were told after the distribution of gifts, the shiny mirrors in which they could see their nakedness, their dark, rubbery genitalia, their snarled and matted wool, the fierce, ropy nipples flaring against the stained, gross coronas of breasts prickled as strawberries, almost the first thing they were told, her shame

110

a story, her story a legend, her legend an apo-
theosis, told through translators or in the broken
pidgins of a thousand tongues, or with actual
hand signs, the complicated history—"There was
this woman, a girl, not even a woman, Mary, the
wife of Joseph, betrothed of Joseph, the union
not consummated, who learned that she was to
bear God's child." "God's?" "Yes. God the Father."
"The father?" "Oh Jesus, our Saviour. Wait. So
this wife, this Mary, a virgin big with child. In a
stable in Bethlehem." "A stable?" "For the horses.
In the straw. In the horses' straw, in the pissed
hay of the cows and camels. And this Mary, this
Virgin, went into labor. You know about labor?
Look, watch. Labor. They were poor. Humble
people. Ragged. Her clothes didn't fit, her shift
was mean, tight across the burden of her belly,
for she couldn't afford to hide what would have
been obvious even in commodious clothing. It
was crowded. The town. People came from all
over to watch her, to stare into her womb where
the fruit was. Strangers. High-ups from great
distances. Shepherds, locals who'd seen the bleed-
ing, dilated cunts of a thousand enceinte dams
but who'd never seen anything like this, an actual
woman on actual straw, writhing not as an animal accustomed to straw would but wildly
thrashing, bucking, not understanding what was
happening to her, not *really*, a virgin, recall, who
not only had never known a man but who had

111

never even touched herself, understand, who wasn't even curious about such things, anything but, and all this in the presence of eyewitnesses, her bewildered husband who knew *he'd* had nothing to do with it, who felt sold if you want to know, and then the Child came, pushing himself, I mean doing the pushing, having to climb up out of that fruity womb practically single-handed because she was still more virgin than mother, more virgin even than woman, who knew nothing of contracting, pressing, pushing, such exercise not only alien to her but obscene. And—" "But if she was still a virgin, how did God the father—" "Well that part's the mystery, but—" —accomplished in a series of filthy, almost humorous gestures broad as actors' that even the missionaries knew, would have to have mastered or actually invent, practicing them like a blasphemous sign language, behind their own backs if they had to, just to make them understand, give them something of the graphic hard-core detail they would almost certainly have to know if their attention was to be engaged later for the theology parts. So she was the Hook. Sex was. The Queen of Heaven. Some Queen. Some Heaven.

Something beyond even repression that the faithful could get past but not she. Not herself. Not Mary. Something beyond even revulsion.

She liked children well enough (though she could never look at one without being reminded of where it had come from, how it had got there, and "Yes," God the Father had beamed, "that's one of the reasons you were chosen") and had even, by her lights, been a good enough mother, though she couldn't have managed without Joseph. Who changed him, cleaned him, Mary—she couldn't help it, she'd have been otherwise if she could—not up to it, unable in her fastidious purity even to wipe his nose or brush his lips with a cloth when he spit up let alone deal with the infant's bowels and urine. If it had been possible she'd have had Joseph nurse it, too. That had been one of her more difficult ordeals, harder for her than the pregnancy, harder than the birth itself, harder even than the Crucifixion (Mary in the limelight too, her pietà postures and public tabloid grief real, felt—she'd loved him, she'd done more, she believed his story, not only mother to the Messiah but his first convert too, her belief antecedent even to Joseph's who'd had a prophecy off an angel, some tout of the Lord, although—who knew?—he may have dismissed the report or, what was more likely, rationalized it, his belief defensive, self-protective, as if it had come from some tout of psychology, while she believed what she believed because the event had only confirmed what her body already knew—though the loss was everyone's by that time, ownerless as hand soap), the nursing terrible for her, her breast offered

113

reluctantly to those cunning lips, the strange, greedy mouth—the poor thing must have been starving; he wouldn't accept the breasts of wet nurses, you couldn't fool it with goat's milk—the nibbling repulsive to her, awful. "Sure," God had said, "that's why I chose you." (Because there was something no one knew, not Joseph, not Jesus, God, of course, though He never spoke of it. It was just that she didn't understand either, as the savages hadn't, as children didn't, the mystery that was beyond the range even of the missionaries, of the popes, of the saints and martyrs. It was how He had done it, how it had been done. She had thought—it was silly, it was crazy, but God didn't draw pictures, He didn't make explanations—she had thought—it was stupid, she was ashamed, she was being alarmist—she thought—it was blasphemous—that the child had done it, that the Christ was somehow father to himself, had fertilized the egg himself, that he'd lived down there always, in the warm female bath, till even the milk he sucked was his own, milk he'd made, first passing it through all the loops and ligatures of her body, the body they shared.)

But she couldn't have done it without Joseph. And that's why *he'd* been chosen, the marriage, as they'd all been then, arranged, made by their parents, the young man timid as herself,

114

with as little desire, more brother than husband, more good friend than brother.

They had never touched each other. Something beyond purity and beyond aversion, too. (What am I? she wondered. What's Joseph?) It had been comfortable to think that they lived under some proscription. It was, she knew, what the world thought. But nothing had been proscribed. The fact was that Joseph was frightened, the fact was that she was.

(She was too old now, of course. But God wasn't. Not Him, not the Lord. He was the Creator and He'd been around the block a few times. With Leda, with Semele, with Alcmene, with Ino and Europa and Danaë. In all His kinky avatars and golden bough Being and beginnings. He was a resourceful lover and came at you as holy livestock or moved in like a front of gilded weather. Who knew but what there wasn't life in the old dog yet?)

So the Queen of Heaven and Joseph, her consort, lived at court under a sort of house arrest. Coming and going in politest society, leashless as God Himself, or Christ, or the Holy Ghost too, given free rein, carte blanche, but neither of them ever testing the waters of that freedom.

They said miracles still happened, that from time to time her statues wept. Why not? She knew how they felt.

115

She summoned a page.

"Ma'am?"

"You're the new boy," said the Holy Mother.

"I'm Flanoy, Ma'am."

"Flanoy, yes. How do you like Heaven, Flanoy?" The cherub flushed. (More places one must not stare, Mary thought. New parts one must avoid. Where the wings were joined to the back. The space they fit into between the shoulder blades when they were retracted. The complicated secret parts of seraphim, cherubim, thrones, dominations, virtues, powers, principalities, archangels and angels, saints, the elect, and all the ordinary saved. Stigmata. One must not look at stigmata. The inner edge of the nimbus. The fabulous scalare of God.) "Not used to us yet?"

"I miss my friends," Flanoy said. "I miss my parents."

"Ah," said the Virgin. "Well, they must be very proud you're here."

"Yes, Ma'am. If they know."

"They're not believers?" Flanoy shifted uneasily. The coverts of his wings thickened with color. "It's all right," said the Virgin Mary, "I've no say in these things."

"I don't know, Ma'am," Flanoy said.

She wanted to say something else to him. She liked to be on good terms with the help.

116

"Well you mustn't be frightened," she said. "Heaven is quite nice really."

"Yes, Ma'am," Flanoy said uncertainly, "it's just that—"

"Yes?"

"It's so *high*."

The Holy Virgin smiled. "Yes. Heaven is very high," she said. "Play something for us please, Flanoy."

"Play?"

"Your music."

"I'm only in the second book of Suzuki."

"Play something for us while we nap," said the Virgin Mother gently.

The child raised his fiddle.

Quiz, in Hell, heard the first faint strains of "Sheep May Safely Graze" and looked in the direction of the music. The others, unaware of it, flared by like tracers, like comets, like shooting stars, like some unquenched astronomy white with reentry. Look at them, Quiz thought. Like teams of horses. Runaways, their harness on fire. No longer in pain himself, he could enjoy the spectacle, their aurora borealtic frenzy and lasered essence charming as fireworks to the appreciative ex-groundskeeper. "Hey," he called, "hey. You guys are beautiful, you know? You look like a World Premier." He laughed. "You

117

look like fucking Chinese New Year's. Come on,"
he said when they snarled at him, "you got to
stop and smell the flowers." One of the damned,
infuriated, came raging to embrace him, use-
lessly attempting to ignite him. "No you don't,"
Quiz said, "it won't work. I'm asbestos now, I'm
cool as a cucumber."

"You're a dud," the tormented man screamed,
"you're a dud," he said, helplessly weeping.

"Yeah," Quiz said, not without kindness,
"I'm a dud. I won't go off."

The lost soul beat at him with his fiery fists,
then, looking at Quiz with wonder, opened his
hands and touched him, not with hatred now
but as if struck by a sudden solace. "What?"
Quiz asked. "What?"

The man smiled and continued to hold him,
relief moving across his face like sunset. "You're
cool," he said. "You're cool. I can douse myself
in you. He's cool," he shouted. "My hands are
cool where I touch him."

"Hey," Quiz said, "hey."

Others moved toward him, groping for space
on his body, desperate to get at least a finger on
him. And "Hey," Quiz called, "hey. There isn't
enough of me. I ain't any Hell's olly olly okshen
free. Let go. Hey. Let go. Hey, get me out of
here," he cried, and suddenly the music was
louder in his head and he felt himself floating
free of Hell. "I'm being translated," he called as

he rose above them, their heat lending him lift, loft, the demon aerodynamics of Hell. He rose. He rose and rose. Climbing the Gothic spaces of the Underworld, floating up beyond the eaves of Hell, carried high impossible distances, escaped as a balloon from the grip of a child.

His stepson had already seen him.

"Pop," Christ said, "how are you?"

The old man shrugged and the boy embraced him, kissed his cheek. "You need anything, Pop? Are they taking care of you?"

"What I need I got," he said.

"So," said the stepson cheerfully, "what's doing, Pop?" The old man made a sly deprecative gesture. "You should have been up there on the Cross with me," he kidded. "No fooling, Pop, I mean it. You've got miles on me long-suffering-wise."

Joseph looked at him steadily, sizing him up, measuring him as he might, in the old days, have measured wood.

"Say it," said the stepson. "Shoot."

"Why should I say it? I said it already a million times. Why should I say it? You like hearing it so much?"

"A million this, a million that. What is it, Pop? That the only number you know?"

"I'm a humble fella. A humble fella says a million he's got in mind maybe six or seven."

"Humble shmumble," said Jesus.

"Tinhorn," said Joseph.

"There you go, Pop. I knew you'd get round to it."

"You started."

"Me?" the Christ said innocently.

"You. You. With your vaudeville Yiddish, your Pop's and What's doing's, your mocky mockery. *You*, Tinhorn, *you*."

"Come on, Pop. Look around. Be a little realistic please."

"Get your legs fixed."

"Here we go," Christ said wearily.

"Get your legs fixed, take a therapy for your hands you shouldn't go in the streets like you have on boxing gloves."

"Pop."

"You wanted to hear it? So hear. You ain't him."

"That's not what He says."

"When the Holy One, Blessed be He, makes a joke He shakes the world with His laughter."

"I'm him, Pop."

"Sure, and I'm the contractor who built this place."

Quiz, in Heaven, feeling good, his felicity only a little tempered by the fact that no one had met him. In life, too, no one had much met him. He'd carried his own suitcases, stopped at the "Y"—not a churchgoer, it was this, he believed, which had saved him, his decision to sleep among Christians at Y.M.C.A.s—seen L.A. and Chicago and other cities from air-conditioned tour buses. Indeed, he had come away from these towns with the vague impression that they had a slightly greenish cast to them. Heaven had no such cast. Heaven was pure light, its palaces and streets, its skies and landscapes primary as acrylic, lustered as lipstick. There was nothing of Hell's dinge or filtered, mitigate shade. It struck him that Heaven was like nothing so much as one of those swell new cities in the Sun Belt—Phoenix, Tucson.

It was a gradual thing, his growing uneasiness. Not much offended at not being met, he nevertheless felt that he'd like to get settled and had determined to start looking around for a "Y" when this cripple came loping up.

"God bless you," said the cripple.

"Sorry, buddy, I don't give handouts," said Quiz, and a magnificent nimbus suddenly bloomed behind the Christ's head like the fanned tail of a peacock.

Quiz, in Heaven, on his knees before the Master, making rapid signs of the cross, his fingers flashing from forehead to breastbone, breastbone to left shoulder, left shoulder to right, boxing the compass, sending pious semaphore.

"Come see God," Christ said, and the man

121

who gave no handouts offered the Saviour his arm and they were in God's throne room and God Himself up on the bench and Quiz all lavish, choreographed humility, prostrate in Moslem effacement, his nose burrowing a jeweled treasury of floor, but put upon, wondering if this were any position for an American, even a dead one, to be in. Barely hearing Christ's words, their meaning slurred by his fear. "—the man You smote . . . redeemed from Hell . . . thought You would want . . . perfect act of contrition."

And Quiz, daring at last to raise his head, to poke it up like someone strafers have made a pass at and missed, marshaling his features, managing to look wounded, injured, aggrieved, forgiving but not quite forgetting.

"You go too far," God told His son.

Because he don't love me, Joseph thought. Because he's adopted. He goes around like that to spite *Him*, to get *His* attention, *His* goat he's after. What do *I* care he ain't perfect? What do I care he ain't him? What a business. We walked around on eggshells with each other, nervous even when we were alone. Sure. Could I watch her undress? Could I hold her in my arms whom the Lord had His eye on? What a business. Because I'm old-fashioned, a zealot of the Lord, and take from Him what a real man wouldn't take from nobody. They call me cuckold and

122

saint me for it. I know what I know if I *don't*
know my rights. He ain't him. I love him, but he
ain't. What can I do but go along if He in His
infinite wisdom Abrahams me and Isaacs the kid,
the one time testing a father, the next a husband? Loyalty oaths He wants, guarantees every
fifty thousand miles. All right, He has them. So
when does He call me in? When does He say
"Well done, good and faithful servant? It was a
hoax, my little two-thousand-year joke. Go home.
Cleave unto Mary. If she'll still have you." What
a business. What a business.

In Hell, Quiz's translation was much dis-
cussed.

"He burnt up."

"He never did. You don't burn up down
here."

"We're eternal lights."

"He flew off. I saw his contrail in what we
have for sky."

"He was never one of us."

"He was an omen," Lesefario said.

"Is that Flanoy? Do you remember me,
Flanoy? It's Mr. Quiz."

"Hi, Mr. Quiz."

"What a shame. A kid like you. Dead as a
doornail, as dodo dead. How'd they get you?
D'you go against? D'you break their rules? Eat

123

too much sweets or touch yourself? Whatcha in for, what's the charge? How'd they get you? Dead to rights?"

"Jesus wants me for a sunbeam."

Lesefario was a thinking man. A long time dead—they had time; they had minutes, seconds, hours, years; what they lacked were calendars, clocks, only the Speidel niceties, digital read-outs, the quartz accounts, only the Greenwich and atomic certainties—he had begun to speculate about the meaning of death. He had never questioned life's meaning. He had assumed it had none. Life was its own gloss. Where conditions changed you didn't look for explanations.

He'd lived in Minnesota, a Minneapolis kid, schoolboy, adult. He'd had his friends and later his cronies. He'd had his shot at stuff, enjoyed much and been disappointed by the rest. He had liked television, a wonderful invention, but had not known when he'd married her that his wife would turn out to be a depressive, a woman who —she couldn't help it, he guessed, but it made things awful and spoiled everything that should have been fun: their trips to restaurants, their cruise to the islands, their daughter's childhood— was never to be pleased by things, who wore her melancholy like a rash. Life had not signified.

Death was another story, so time-consuming—they had time—so draining, demanding, taking not just his but all their attentions, given over to pain, not causeless sadness like his wife's but to a suffering like Wallenda stagefright, to not knowing from one moment to the next—they had time—whether what had to be endured and would be endured even *could* be endured. Death made no sense but it meant something.

When Lesefario formulated this last proposition he decided that he must try to save them, to become heroic in Hell who had been a clerk in a Minneapolis liquor store in a red-lined neighborhood, who had opened up in the morning always a little scared of the winos around the entrance, always a little scared of the blacks, always a little scared of people who asked him to cash their checks, always a little scared of teenagers, of minors who showed him phony I.D. cards, of the big, beefy delivery men, of customers, of anyone who would come into a liquor store.

What could *he* do he asked himself, and why should he do it? Who was he, stuck away down here, stashed for the duration in some nameless base camp of Hell, a thoughtful fraidycat formerly in the liquor trade, or, no, not *even* the liquor trade, a clerk in the making change trade, whose last human contact would be, had been, with the trigger-happy jerk Lesefario had known was coming for fifteen years? And so scared he knew—because he knew as soon as the guy came

through the door he was the last human being
he'd ever see, trying to size him up though fear
hurt his eyes and Lesefario lost his face like a
center fielder a ball in the sun—that even if he
lived he would never be able to pick the thug out
of a lineup. Acknowledging even in that first
brief bruised view of him all that he and his
murderer—did they get good reviews? were their
names household words? was their health all
it should be, or their children top-drawer?—had
in common, and if this was the fellow, and if this
was it, why shouldn't the killer be made to feel
the force of that astonishing fact?

"If you're all I have for deathbed—" Lesefario had said.

"Wha?"

"—then I want your attention. I guess most
folks die out of their element, D.O.A.'d by circumstance and only—"

"Hey you, no tricks."

"—the night shift in attendance."

"No tricks I said. Hands high and shut up."

"Because—"

"I'm going to have to teach you a lesson,"
the killer said, and cut him down before he could
teach the killer one, his last word "because" in a
life he'd already decided didn't make sense. And
a good thing, too, Lesefario thought, groping for
the last words he still couldn't formulate, that
given months, years, he could not finally have

put together. (Though he had an idea they would have been simple. Why had he wanted to make the point that he would have been fifty-two years old on his next birthday?) So who in hell—ha ha, he thought—was *he*, who had missed out on life's, to discover death's meaning, or to try to save them? Just who in hell did he think he was—the Christ of the Boonies?

So he grabbed the first one he saw, stinging him with his temperature.

"Aargh," the fellow shrieked, pushing Lesefario off.

"It's all right," Lesefario said from where he had fallen in Hell. "It's all right. Listen to me. Are you listening? It's Four fifty-three P.M., Tuesday, June 27th, Seven thousand, eight hundred four."

"Say what?"

"The time. Quiz told me the time when he was translated. I've been keeping track."

"The time?"

"Four fifty-*four*. Yes. It's too big a job for one man. Tell the others. We've got to keep track."

"Why?"

"Hurry. (Twelve one hundredths, thirteen one hundredths, fourteen one hundredths)—Please! (Sixteen one hundredths.)"

"Why do we have to know the time?"

"Don't argue. Because the meaning of death

—(Twenty one hundredths. And start again one
hundredths)—The meaning of death is how long
it takes."

Quiz was a queer, funny man, Flanoy thought.
Still, he might be all right or he wouldn't be here,
would he? He'd been down in Hell with the
bad men. Was it a sin not to like an angel? He'd
ask Mother Mary. Maybe he'd tell her some
of the wicked things he'd done. Still, he thought,
he'd better not say anything that could get Mr.
Quiz in trouble. He was the only one who'd
known Flanoy.

He knew me when I lived. He heard me
laugh, he saw me throw.

In Hell they were chanting the time. The
Bakhtiari nomads were chanting, the Finns were
chanting. Frenchmen chanted in French, Dutch-
men in Dutch. All over Hell the billions who had
died, each in his own mnemonic way, sometimes
to himself, often aloud, uttered the special syl-
lables he'd learned would fill up seconds. "Michi-
gan hydrangeas, Cleveland for its tea," a woman
from the Australian Outback said, while her
companion, a performing dwarf for Spanish mer-
cenaries, kept a silent, running tab.

Ellerbee was chanting too. "Heaven is a
theme park," he tolled, "May was once my wife."

Lesefario, who had given a downbeat which was already obsolete by the time it reached a party of Greek skiers killed in avalanche and actual days behindhand when it got to a Soviet film star dead of a fever on a trip to Japan, declared he was in contact with Quiz, that though their techniques were primitive he received periodic corrections from Quiz, himself in communication with the sacred authorities, pleading their case, an eyewitness, he told them, to their Devil's Island circumstance—an eyewitness, a brother. They must keep counting, Lesefario said.

"Two A.M. Sunday, July 10th, Seven thousand, eight hundred four. (Four one hundredths, five one hundredths, six one hundr—) Count, *count,* it's Houston Control here. The state of the art isn't so hot yet, but so long as we keep counting we'll get corrections from Quiz. Count, any second may be the last."

"What's that? Astrology?" said this ancient denizen of Hell.

"No, no," Lesefario said feelingly. "It's important."

"I've seen it all and it's just another fad," the tortured man said. "It's some self-help, do-it-yourself scam. It don't mean shit. Crazy Ellerbee had us praying, knees bowed in brimstone. *Praying!* Turned Hell into bloody Sunday school. 'Sacred authorities' my third-degree burns!" And Lese-fario wondered: Ellerbee? Is that my Ellerbee? Is Ellerbee dead? In hell?

"(Eighteen one hundredths, nineteen one hundredths—)" (But not even his own heart in it, his flash-in-the-pan hopes and heroics extin-guished, though he would probably keep count-ing awhile—they had time—someone trying to keep a rally alive, a plant in an audience milking ovation, a guy at a party gone sour suggesting the song which would bring them together again.)

"Mother Mary?"
"Yes, Flanoy?"
"Was Jesus lonely?"
"Lonely?"
"Because he didn't have brothers. Because he didn't have sisters."
"I don't think he was lonely."
"Were there kids to play with?"
"It was so long ago. I hardly remember."
"You could do lots of stuff in the desert. It'd be just like the beach."
"Yes?"
"You could go barefoot. You could bury kids in the sand. With a pail of water from the oasis you could make things. Did Jesus do that stuff?"
"I hardly remember."

"Maybe he didn't have anyone to play with. Maybe that's why you don't remember."

"He worked with his father. He helped his father."

"His father?"

"He helped my husband," Mary said, blushing.

Flanoy nodded. "Back home there was always plenty to do."

"Do you miss being home?"

"I miss my mother," Flanoy said.

"Oh, Flanoy," Mary said, and held out her arms.

The Virgin comforted the sobbing child. She cupped the back of Flanoy's head in her large soft hand. His legs, between her knees, his small, slim body pressed against her bosom, made a discrete, comfortable weight. Mary, touched by the child's sweet, ultimate homesickness, reached around him and took all his weight now, gathering the little boy onto her lap, both their bodies shedding angle, temperature and impediment resolved into the soft symbiotics of need and competence, the tongue and groove aptitudes of love.

This is heresy, she thought, indifferent to the idea, and hugged him closer, all her supple maternals alive, returned from helplessness, fetched back intact two thousand years. Soon his body will begin to bite, she thought, his tears to chafe, yet she made no adjustments, no move to kiss him off with a final squeeze. It was not even a pietà, no long, lame lapful. Literally, she cradled him in her arms, his knees near his chest, as one might carry a child high up in water.

"Better?" she asked.

"Yes, Ma'am."

He climbed down from her lap and seated himself cross-legged beside her like a child in short pants. She stroked his head, her fingers trailing a forgetful, comfortable doodle in his fine hair. She dozed.

Christ was there, Joseph was. Flanoy was gone.

"Where's the child?" she asked.

"Flanoy? Gone off," her son said.

"He's a good boy."

"You're good *to* him, Madonna. I was in time for the tableau."

"He wanted to know if you had playmates. He wanted to know if you were lonely."

"Who is this kid, Mary?" her husband asked. "What do we know about him anyway?"

"His name's Flanoy," she told him wearily. "He's from Minnesota. He's dead."

"Big deal. Who ain't dead?"

"Mother is comfortable with the dead."

"With you maybe not so comfortable," Joseph said. "Bamboozler. Do you know how tired the woman gets? What a strain? Come clean, why don't you? Admit you ain't him."

"Please, Joseph. I have a mouth."

"You got a mouth? Use it. Tell him. Go on. What, you're so crazy about these people it makes a difference he ain't Messiah?"

"Oh, please," Christ said.

"Both of you," Mary said.

"You're tired," Joseph said. "He woke you. This one. Your son, the magic cripple, who bumps into things."

"Both of you, please," Mary said.

"We're going," Joseph said. "Get some rest."

"Flanoy," she called softly when they had gone, "Flanoy—"

Who no longer brought his violin, she noticed, who came now whenever she felt need of him, who seemed to feel her need even before she did, who anticipated it and suddenly appeared and climbed into her lap and asked about them, questions about Jesus, about Joseph, herself, things not in the Bible, how she'd felt when she found out who her son was, if they'd taken vacations together as his family had, if it was always religious, if she'd heard from Jesus when he was in the wilderness all that time, whether she'd believed she'd see him again after they killed him, and trading his history for hers, filling her in on the world, if only his limited experience of it, but knowing more real history from his brief decade on earth than she knew for all her millennia in the sky, and what *could* she know, Flanoy asked —did history say its prayers?—did she know the slaves had been freed, or the names of state capitals, did she know there was television now, movies—he told her movies he'd seen, breaking her heart as he recounted sad stories about children, their animals, faithful dogs and noble horses, how the children had to put them away themselves when they were injured, the lessons they'd learned, and making her laugh when he told her the comedies—saying, though she knew all about this, how loved she was, how honored, winning her over, as she did him, with confidences, telling his secrets, climbing on her lap as he grew tired, his soft, comfortable body almost meant to be there—and now maybe Jesus had a right to be jealous—and all manner of things spoken of which she had never spoken of, and one day bringing his violin. "I've been practicing," he said shyly, and played to perfection grand compositions she had never heard, even in Heaven.

"Why, you're so good," she said, surprised.

"Yes," he said. "I don't know where it comes from. I think I'm inspired," and played a melody that left them both in tears, the child so wracked by the beauty that he could not finish.

"Come," she said, "sit in my lap."

And Flanoy climbed up and Mary held him,

the lovely melody still echoing somewhere in memory, the both of them still listening. "Ah," she said. "Ah," sighed Flanoy. And afterwards, in the stillness—as if they both heard together not only the melody but when it had stopped— Flanoy asked his question.

"Was it like that?"

"What?"

"When God— You know."

"When God?"

He toyed with the collar of her gown, his gentle fingers lightly tracing the line of her throat, and it was as if she blossomed itch just as he assuaged it, need just as he answered it.

"When God put Jesus in you?"

"When *God*—?"

"Do you know how He did it? Did you know it was Him? I mean you were a virgin, did you never suspect?"

"*You*," she screamed. She flung him from her lap.

"But what did *I* do?"

"You're at me again. Wasn't one time enough?"

"What did I do?" Flanoy asked, crying. "I didn't do anything. What did I do?" he sobbed, and ran from the room.

"*I'm carrying His child!*" shrieked the Virgin Mary.

❊   ❊   ❊

God gave a gala, a levee at the Lord's.

All Heaven turned out. "Gimme," He said, "that old time religion." His audience beamed. They cheered, they ate it up. They nudged each other in Paradise. "What did I tell you?" He demanded over their enthusiasm. "It's terrific, isn't it? I told you it would be terrific. All you ever had to do was play nice. Are you disappointed? Is this Heaven? Is this God's country? In your wildest dreams—let Me hear it. Good—in your wildest dreams, did you dream such a Treasury, this museum Paradise? Did you dream My thrones and dominions, My angels in fly-over? My seraphim disporting like dolphins, tumbling God's sky in high Heaven's high acrobacy? Did you imagine the miracles casual as card tricks, or ever suspect free lunch could taste so good? They should see you now, eh? They should see you now, trembling in rapture like neurological rut. Delicious, correct? Piety a la mode! That's it, that's right. Sing hallelujah! Sing Hizzoner's hosannas, Jehovah's gee whiz! Well," God said, "that's enough, that will do." He looked toward the Holy Family, studying them for a moment. "Not like the crèche, eh?" He said. "Well is it? *Is* it?" He demanded of Jesus.

"No," Christ said softly.

"No," God said, "not like the crèche. Just look at this place—the dancing waters and indirect lighting. I could put gambling in here, off-track betting. Oh, oh, My costume jewelry ways, My game show vision. Well, it's the public. You've got to give it what it wants. Yes, Jesus?"

"Yes," Jesus said.

"It just doesn't look lived in, is that what you think?"

"Call on someone else," Christ said.

"Sure," God said. "I'm Hero of Heaven. I call on Myself."

That was when He began His explanations. He revealed the secrets of books, of pictures and music, telling them all manner of things—why marches were more selfish than anthems, lieder less stirring than scat, why landscapes were to be preferred over portraits, how statues of women were superior to statues of men but less impressive than engravings on postage. He explained why dentistry was a purer science than astronomy, biography a higher form than dance. He told them how to choose wines and why solos were more acceptable to Him than duets. He told them the secret causes of inflation—"It's the markup," He said—and which was the best color and how many angels could dance on the head of a pin. He explained why English was the first language at Miss Universe pageants and recited highlights from the eighteen-minute gap.

Mary, wondering if she showed yet, was glad Joseph was seated next to her. Determined to look proud, she deliberately took her husband's hand. So rough, she thought, such stubby fingers.

He explained why children suffered and showed them how to do the latest disco steps. He showed them how to square the circle, cautioning afterwards that it would be wrong.

He revealed the name of Kennedy's assassin and told how to shop for used cars.

Why He's talking to *me*, Quiz thought. These other folks couldn't ever have had any use for this stuff. He's talking to *me*. Quiz was right, but He had something for everyone. He was unloading, giving off wisdom like radioactivity, plumbing the mysteries, and now His voice was reasonable, not the voice of a grandfather but of a king, a chief, someone unelectable, there always, whose very robes and signals of office were not expensive or even rare so much as *His*, as if He wore electricity or mountain range or clothed Himself in waterfall. He explained—"I am the Manitou, too" —how the rain dance worked. They were charmed. He described how He had divided the light from the darkness on the morning of the first day. They were impressed. He demonstrated how He had done Hell. They were awed.

"You have wondered," He said, "why things are as they are. You have wondered, you have speculated. You have questioned My motives." Groans of denial went up from the saints. He ignored them. " 'Why,' the philosophers ask, 'so piecemeal? Why His fits and starts theology, His stop and go arrangements? Can't He make up His mind? Why the carrot, why the stick? Why the evenings and mornings of those consecutive days? Why only after first fashioning them could He see that they were good? Why, having landscaped an Eden, having leached and prepared the precious pious soils, having His fell swoop harvests and sweet successful bumper crops, did He need the farmer and plant the man, set him upright, a scarecrow essence in the holy field? Why first an Adam then an Eve, or Eve at all, or if an Eve why torn from that depleted man who, image of his maker once removed removes again to blur the reciprocities in that deserving girl? Why a serpent, why a tree? Why fine print at all so near the start of things? Why codicils and conditions, all that lawyerly qualm? Why strings? Why that Miranda decision hocus mumbo jumbo pocus, reading rights to a man and a woman who not only do not know that they are already in trouble but do not even know what trouble is? And ain't exile cruel and unusual punishment when there's no place to go?

"'Of course they fell. Who wouldn't fall in such a place? Who wouldn't fall where the gravity was a thousand and two in just the shade? Who wouldn't fall when the thickest crop in that garden was just gravity?'"

Flanoy had come out of his sulk. He smiled but Mother Mary would not look at him. Gosh, he thought, one moment comforted in Mother Mary's lap, the next tumbled, spilled, knocked from it as one might clumsy milk.

" 'Adam and Eve on the rock pile now, the chain gang. Working off their offense and raising kids, extra hands, till it was all cultivated now, if not a peaceable kingdom then at least a trained one, the old indebtedness paid up like mortgage. And then a flood. A *flood!* The whole earth disaster area. The spoiled corn and wetted wheat, the fruit and flooded fields all mash and only Father Noah's ark afloat in all that liquorish sea, sailing the farms, cruising the ruined hectares, versts and acreage, and Noah unclear, everyone unclear, about the nature of the charges this time, the actual straw that broke the actual camel's back unspecified.' " —Yes, Flanoy thought, with me, too, and moved closer to Quiz— " 'And then the covenant again, the old instrument which by this time even man knew was the only way God ever did business, never just by handshake let alone by the binding, even honored, nod or raised finger or tickled ear which perhaps only the auctioneer ever sees and which, nevertheless, always seems to be good enough even for him, but a contract, a compact, something a little more official than trust and less flimsy than faith, yet not an actual

140

agreement at all and even the single simple seeming layman's conditions—"Behave, play nice, be good"—and down home language a pitch beyond understanding.

" 'Reprieved from oceans. Starting over. Breaking clean. Almost sophisticated now, almost used to it, a kind of emigré, Ellis Islanded, the culture not so shocking, for all were greenhorns, greenhorns everywhere, and you'd think that maybe the ironic point of all this vagabondage was just to keep folks busy, hold them still.' "

Sh'ma Yisroel Adonoi Elohenu, Adonoi Echod, Joseph mumbled. He pounded his breast with the hand that had just been resting in Mary's.

He looks like someone driving nails, Christ thought.

" 'A tinker God, you'd think, Someone editorial, nuts for amendment. Or even God at all, do you suppose, with His second and third chances, His governor's fond delight in commutation, reprieve? A father indeed, a daddy, a pop, Who counts to three perhaps, gets past two and goes to fractions—"Two and a half, two and three quarters, four fifths . . ."

" 'Fond of mountains, a thing for heights. Ararat, Sinai. (Who ever delighted in the nature He had made, crouching perhaps, making frames of His hands, scouting location like a director, His shingle hung in garden, ocean, wilderness,

141

and the higher elevations, a sort of majestic Fop posed on postcard and practicing His Law only where there was a view, never on just ordinary earth.)

" 'Another covenant. This time in writing. Elegant, He may have thought, powerful but elegant, and showed man something in a stone tablet. (Who worked always in His chosen mediums— earth, water, fire. Moses on the mountain would be air.) The terms terminal, one through ten. (Who was God again now He could get past three.) Dealing always, note, with leaders, as He had dealt with Points of Interest, oblique angle, off-center prospect, steep vision like a goat's purchase, His summit conferees the elect of earth, its leading men, God's chosen persons, ho ho ho. And Moses not two minutes at sea level but the people He had never deigned to deal with directly were at it again, doing the golden calf like a new dance. And Moses outraged as God at their loose talk and their sweet tooth for leeks and garlic, Egypt's spectacular shade.

" 'But what did He do? Nothing. As always. Nothing. Who made the world in six days and flooded it in forty but couldn't count to three— Wait. Wait. *Nothing. Nothing!*

" 'Unless you count a covenant. "I'll give you Christ," as if to say. "Just pledge belief. If being good was hard, forget it, just pledge belief. Believe." ' "

Most of them were praying now. Even Mary had lowered her head, as Joseph had though he had ceased to sway, whose strident orthodoxy had bleached to something almost episcopal, who stood bareheaded, his yarlmulke fallen, and in phylacteries undone as laces.

"So," God said, "what do you make of Me, eh? What do you make of Me now you understand that finally it takes two to break a contract as well as to make one? What do you make of Me Who could have gotten it all right the first time, saved everyone trouble and left Hell unstocked? Do you love Me? Do you forgive and forget as easily as I do? Do you?"

Mother Mary peeked at the fluted piping of His nimbus, the sacred, secret rim, like icing on pastry, where the helix tucked into His golden head. She held her belly in her hands and hoped this one would be a girl.

"*Do* you?"

"Yes," they cried. "Yes!"

"Why do I do it then? Why?"

"So we might choose," said one of the saved.

"What? Speak up."

"So we might choose."

"Never," God thundered. "What do I care for the sanctity of your will? Never!"

"Goodness," a saint shouted. "You get off on goodness."

"On goodness? *Me?*" God laughed. "On goodness? Is that what you think? Is that what you think? Were you born yesterday? You've been in the world. Is that how you explain trial and error, history by increment, God's long Slap and Tickle, His Indian-gift wrath? *Goodness?* No. It was Art! It was always Art. I work by the contrasts and metrics, by beats and the silences. It was all Art. *Because it makes a better story is why.*"

Christ held up his damaged hands. "It makes a better story?" He was furious. "Because it makes a better *story?* Is this true? *Is* it?"

"Sure it's true," God said. Then, pausing, He saw Quiz hold back a yawn. "—teen one hundredths," He said, "nineteen one hundredths, *twenty* one hundredths. All right, that's it! *Kairos!* Doomsday!"

Lesefario, in Hell, did not know at first that he had stopped burning. He thought pain's absence some new pain, something eye of the hurricane or the heavy peace before the firing squad takes aim. He shook himself. He seemed, like the scabbed and crusted others, like an animal, a bear perhaps, after winter's long somnolence. Instinct, memory, did not work that fast. It needed its bearings and landmarks, it required its surveyors' grapples, some alphabet of location.

"How long? How long did it take?" asked the fellow who'd told him his counting was a fad.

"What? How long?"

"Death. How long did it take?"

"I stopped counting," he said.

"Shame," the man said.

"Yes," said Lesefario, his heart breaking.

Bodies rose to the surface of the seas and began swimming. They were released from faded, colorless flags, stove ships, hidden pilings where they had snagged for years. They came up out of shoals and split sandbars. The drowned and murdered floated up from the bottoms of lakes, their faces and bodies in the same dishabille in which they had died. They seeped out of riverbanks, they surfaced in wells. A rising tide of the dead.

In woods and rain forests they quickened, corpses lost years. They came to in deserts, they waked up on mountains, a treasury of jigsaw death. One could not have suspected their numbers, that so many random had fallen. These were merely the discards, the old boot dead, stochastic as beer can, deposit bottle.

They woke up in battlefields. They gathered themselves where they had exploded. They got up in hospitals, their deaths not yet discovered. They still wore identification bracelets, I.V.s dangled from their wrists like slack banderillas. They woke up in archeology, cities done in by earthquake, fire, and time. They climbed out of caves, out of canyons, geology.

Up out of mine shafts they came, comrades in cave-ins.

They worked their way through holes they had melted in glaciers.

All earth gave up its dead.

They strained against coffin lids, against sealers. Stymied as escape artists they banged encumbrance. They swarmed, they popped through, the hatched, frantic chicks of death.

A man named Ladlehaus climbed out of his grave like someone backing out a window.

Like elopers they left their burials. They touched their tombs and niches as if they were the old rooms of childhood, brushing them lightly, as if they were dusting. They scrutinized their plots and read their markers like people hunting addresses. They loitered in their graveyards as if they were keeping appointments. Already they missed their deaths. There were complaints. They were cold in just sunlight after the heat of Hell. Those who had donated organs had lost them forever. They could feel the cavities and hollows, the terrible gouged and amputate absentness. A woman who had given her eyes away stirred her fingers in her weeping holes. "So grotesque," she moaned, "death grotesque as life. All, all grotesque."

They came down from churchyards on hillsides and in from cemeteries on the outskirts of town. They bestirred themselves in the celebrated tombs and sepulchers of the big-shot dead.

Their bodies shone with gore like wet paint. They sooted the world as if it were carpet. The living and dead were thrown together, and the dead looked away first.

Tribes covered the earth now, families did, clans, races. Mary, squeamish in the press of population, could not bear the stench. It's morning sickness, she told herself. Joseph couldn't get over how much things had changed, and Christ flinched when he saw soldiers. Quiz, looking for sanctuary, pulled Flanoy into a Y.M.C.A.

Into the Valley of Jehoshaphat they came and along all the coasts of Palestine. They covered the ranges of Samaria and Judea, of Abilene and Gilead, and stood in the Plains of Jezreel and Sharon and spread out by Kinnereth's Sea and the salted waters between Idumea and Moab. And were a million deep all about the tough shores of the ruined Mediterranean circle.

They seemed a kind of vegetation, their burnt skin a smear of sullen growth. Pressed together, Coney Island'd, Woodstock'd, Tivoli Garden'd, Jonestown'd, they seemed spectators at some gameless stadium, vast as the world.

They waited. They did not know what was going to happen. They consulted the religious among them but they didn't know either.

Then God was there and, strangely, all could

see Him. There was not a bad seat in the house.

It was short and sweet.

"Because I never found My audience," God said. "Because I never found My audience." He looked at the assembled dead, at the living billions anxious at ground zero. "You gave me, some of you, your ooh's and aah's, the Jew's hooray and Catholic's Latin deference—all theology's pious wow. But I never found My audience." He looked at Mary, who had feared Him, victim to His blue ribbon force, distrustful still, savoring the ordinary who had been taken out of all that. "I never found My audience. What had you," He asked His audience, "to complain of? You had the respect of peers. You *had* peers." He looked at Jesus. "You were no audience. You had all the advantages. You were only God's clone." And at Joseph. "You were a carpenter," He said. "You did things with your hands. Why didn't you admire Me more?" At the damned. "I gave you pain. Do you appreciate the miracle? To make it up out of thin air, deep, free-fall space, the gifted, driven atoms of remonstrance? Trickier than orange juice or the taste of Brie. Because I never found My audience," said God and annihilated, as Mother Mary and Christ and Lesefario and Flanoy and Quiz in their Y.M.C.A. seafront room in Piraeus and all Hell's troubled sighed, *everything*.